LONG RIDER

SNAKETOWN

CLAY DAWSON

16

DIAMOND BOOKS, NEW YORK

SNAKETOWN

A Diamond Book / published by arrangement with
the author

PRINTING HISTORY
Diamond edition / September 1991

All rights reserved.
Copyright © 1991 by Charter Communications, Inc.
This book may not be reproduced in whole or in part, by
mimeograph or any other means, without permission.
For information address: The Berkley Publishing Group,
200 Madison Avenue, New York, New York 10016

ISBN: 1-55773-586-7

Diamond Books are published by The Berkley Publishing Group,
200 Madison Avenue, New York, New York 10016.
The name "DIAMOND" and its logo are trademarks
belonging to Charter Communications, Inc.

PRINTED IN THE UNITED STATES OF AMERICA

10 9 8 7 6 5 4 3 2 1

CHAPTER ONE

The tall man stalked quickly across the crowded wharf, making his way through a maze of barrels and crates, piles of green lumber and fat sacks of grain. A wagonload of hides rolled by. Black roustabouts hurried along, their broad backs straining under heavy bars of iron and kegs of nails. A raw mix of waterfront smells hung in the humid morning air—horse droppings, Red River mud, grease, wood-smoke, and tar. Hours before, a teamster in a hurry had lost a wheel and dumped hundreds of tomatoes and melons on the wharf. The driver cursed his mules, repaired the broken wheel, and left the produce there to rot. The mess added to the odor of the docks and drew great clouds of flies.

If Gabe Conrad noticed the clutter and the smell, he clearly paid them no mind. His long legs took him quickly toward the forest of masts and derricks and high black smokestacks that rose above the Shreveport wharves. Nearly a dozen riverboat steamers were nosed inshore, fighting for loading space. Gabe studied the fancy-lettered names on the stern-wheelers' sides: *Red River Star*, *Caddo Lady*, *Bayou Queen*. The name he wanted wasn't there. He slapped at a fly on his cheek and moved along.

As Gabe walked by, a striking young woman watched him with more than passing interest. Her husband was looking the other way, talking to a friend about cottonseed and corn. Men often noticed Gabe Conrad. They sensed he was different, that he didn't quite belong. They saw the worn cartridge belt strapped around his waist, the Colt hanging loosely in a holster, butt facing out. They noticed he didn't smile when he should, that he didn't seem to hear you when you spoke. He wasn't a man you'd pick to tell a joke you'd heard in Cheyenne or stop to share a moment of idle talk.

Women, however, saw something more in Gabe. The girl on the dock studied his sun-darkened skin, the straight sweep of sandy hair beneath the black slouch hat. A worn linen duster reached clear to Gabe's low-heeled Army boots, but the garment failed to hide the muscled shoulders and lean, wiry frame.

The young woman wondered what lay behind the pale, almost colorless gray eyes. The eyes, the mouth, the firm set of the jaw gave nothing away. Yet, to a woman who'd known a man or two, these features said a great deal. This was a man you couldn't tame—and wouldn't much care to if you could. A girl would never know where she stood with such a man, but she'd never be bored when he happened to drop around.

The woman smiled to herself. A thought touched the edge of her mind and made her blush. She reached out and gripped her husband's arm. The man she had was just fine. He didn't have pale gray eyes, but he'd stay where he belonged—and that was something, too.

The sharp blast of a whistle cut the air. Gabe moved past a pyramid of crates and spotted black smoke rising down the way. A roustabout standing nearby guessed his thoughts.

"If you want the *Cypress Moon*, that's her," the man said. "Just gettin' under way."

Gabe nodded his thanks, gripped his pack, and hurried on. The *Cypress Moon* shuddered as the twin stacks belched another choking cloud of smoke. As Gabe crossed the gangway, the whistle shrieked again. A seaman showed Gabe a surly look and hauled the narrow plank aboard. Other men shouted across

the decks, and the lines snaked free.

The captain's not a man for long good-byes, Gabe thought. He walked from the bow to the stern and dropped his pack on the deck. The stern-wheeler backpaddled slowly away from shore. The engines clattered loudly, churning up the brick-colored silt that gave the Red River its name. Then, for an instant, the engines nearly came to a halt. The paddle wheels stopped, the engines caught again, and the *Cypress Moon* labored upstream.

Several other passengers stood by the railing, looking out over the river. A group of merchants complained about prices in the East. Past them, an elderly man in a tailored frock coat and a blue silk vest stood alone. Gabe thought he had to be close to eighty, but he was still as tall and straight as an aging pine. A full head of silver hair was visible under a broad-brimmed planter's hat. He had a well-trimmed beard and thick white brows. Piercing blue eyes squinted at the river past a nose that would make an eagle proud. Deep lines etched the corners of his mouth, drawing his lips into a permanent smile that said, "I've seen about everything there is."

A gambler, Gabe decided, and a good one at that. Likely made enough money on the river to buy St. Louis once or twice.

The man seemed to sense Gabe's presence. Turning from the river, he looked right at Gabe, held his eyes a moment, nodded, and looked away. Gabe felt as if someone had slipped a cold blade between his ribs. The strange feeling startled him, made him turn swiftly to see if someone was standing near. He felt like a fool; the chill that had touched him went away, but whatever he had seen in the old man's eyes was still there. He was certain he'd seen the man before—and just as sure their paths had never crossed.

It didn't make sense. Something was there, Gabe knew. He could follow the thought and see where it might go. But something warned him there were answers here he didn't want to know, a trail he didn't want to find.

Let it go, he told himself. Whatever it is, it'll stay or go away. He was thirsty and wondered where he might get a drink. The cabins on a boat this size would likely be upstairs.

There'd be some kind of galley on the deck where he was standing right now.

Gabe started forward, then stopped. A shout went up to port near the stern. At first, Gabe thought surely one of the passengers had fallen in. He walked back a few yards, looked, and saw a stout, bald-headed man in an English-cut suit, yelling at the woman by his side. Veins stood out on his brow, and his features were dark with rage. He clenched his fists and leaned in close, giving the poor woman what for. The woman was small and fine-boned and somewhat younger than the man. Abuse had robbed her of her spirit and her looks. The beauty was there somewhere, but the woman no longer let it show. As Gabe watched, she gazed out over the river and took the man's verbal lashing without a fight. Her face showed no expression, no emotion of any kind. This was clearly her defense. She wasn't there; she was somewhere else. Somewhere the man couldn't go.

Gabe tightened his hands on the railing. He felt nothing but contempt for such a man. The bastard had taken everything the woman had to give and left her with nothing but her fear.

The incident touched Gabe deeply. Cowardice and dishonor were qualities he despised. Gabe had been born of white parents, but raised around Oglala council fires. He had found strong values there, lessons he could never forget. All white men were not cowards—no one but a fool would say that. Gabe was white himself, and he knew many whites who were extremely courageous men. Still, the ways of the Lakota were the ways of his spirit. He was Gabe Conrad, but he was also Long Rider. The name had been given to him by the Oglala Sioux. He had earned it in his fourteenth year, after he had ridden two horses to death to warn a Lakota camp of a raid by cavalry troops.

And now, when he saw the man shouting at the woman on the deck of the *Cypress Moon*, attacking someone who could not defend herself, it was Long Rider, and not Gabe Conrad, who put the words "white man" and "coward" together in a single harsh image that burned like a brand within his soul.

"Cavalry" was a part of that image as well. He had ridden to save a village from a cavalry attack. And, a few years after

that, it was a cavalry officer who had shot Gabe's Oglala wife and run his mother through with a saber. Both of these horrors had occurred before Gabe's very eyes.

The image wasn't a fair one, Gabe knew. Still, it was there, a part of the Oglala spirit of his youth. He could not cast that spirit aside and had no desire to do so.

Gabe looked away from the couple and tried to put them out of his mind. Picking up his pack, he made his way forward past the high stacks of cargo and the noisy sound of the boiler. The *Cypress Moon* had rounded a bend and left Commerce Street and the busy wharves of Shreveport behind. With the stern-wheeler well under way, a faint breeze stirred the muggy air, keeping the mosquitoes at bay.

Gabe paused a moment, then climbed the short staircase to the hurricane deck. Turning to port, he passed one of the tall, twin stacks and walked aft. The number on his cabin said "3." Gabe gripped the knob and then paused. The tall, white-haired man he'd seen on the deck below now appeared at the top of the stairs. Gabe gave the old gambler a wary look.

"Morning to you, sir." The man touched the brim of his hat and offered Gabe his hand. Gabe was relieved. He met the man's eyes, and there was nothing peculiar there at all.

"Name's Lucas Harrow. If you're in Number Three, I would guess we're neighbors for the trip."

"Gabe Conrad," said Gabe. "I guess we are." He wasn't surprised that the old man's grip was firm and sure. Closer, he could see his first appraisal was on the nose. The man was strong despite his years. He was only an inch or two shorter than Gabe's six-two; his eyes were clear as mountain ice, and there was no hesitation in his walk.

"Unfortunate affair," Harrow said. He frowned and shook his head, nodding down below. "Most *un*fortunate affair. Man like that should be taken out and horsewhipped, I say. Yes, sir. Taken out and whipped."

"I reckon so," Gabe said. He looked past Harrow, showing as little interest as he could. What should or shouldn't be done about the man was idle talk—unless you meant to do the thing

yourself. And if you did, that's what you'd do, and there was nothing to discuss.

"Summer is the worst time to travel there is," Harrow said. He drew a dark cheroot from his vest, struck a lucifer on the wall, and lit up. "The bugs are bad and the water stinks, and nothing but ugly women come aboard. Pretty girls stay home and drink iced lemonade. This your first time on the river, might I ask?"

"First time on this one," Gabe said. "I've been up one or two."

"Well, then we share that fact in common. I have traveled up a few hot and odorous waterways myself." Harrow swept his arm in a circle that took in everything from Africa to the poles. "Going up to Jefferson for business or pleasure? Hope to hell it's business—not a whole lot of pleasure up there. Used to be, but there isn't anymore. Place has gone to pot. Where was I? Oh, right. Adventure lies up the river, I'll tell you sure. Either that, or total boredom, sir. *To*tal boredom, as you've never experienced it before. Sometimes a man finds wonder and good companionship. At others, nothing but disaster. Overpriced whiskey and overage whores."

Gabe had to smile. "I'd believe you've done a little traveling, Mr. Harrow. I truly would."

Lucas Harrow flicked a spot of soot off his coat. Gabe could tell that he was pleased. "Shows, does it? Well, by God, it should. Been up the Muddy so many times, ought to have paddles on my feet instead of toes. I've eaten so many catfish I—"

Harrow suddenly stopped. He frowned and looked away, studying the tip of his cheroot. He looked at the cross-draw rig at Gabe's waist, the worn-down heels of his boots.

"By God, I reckon if you act like a fool long enough, you're goin' to start being one for sure," Harrow said. He looked soberly at Gabe. "A man gets used to the part he's got to play, Mr. Conrad. Cards and fancy talk is what I do; I don't have to tell you that. You aren't any drummer on your first trip west of Buffalo. You're not much lookin' to lose your gold watch or hear a lot of riverboat lies. Knew that the minute you came aboard, but my mouth got the jump on my brain, and

I'm sorry 'bout that. If you'll allow me, sir, I'd sure like to buy you a drink when the heat goes out of the day."

"Fine, maybe so," Gabe said. He hefted his pack and opened the cabin door.

"Well, then." Harrow smiled, standing directly in Gabe's path. "I suppose we'll be seeing one another at the noonday meal. Won't be anything to write home about—never saw a riverboat cook didn't drink to some excess. I recall a trip up to Fort Benton. The *Delta Queen* it was—"

"Been a pleasure," Gabe said shortly. He slipped past the gambler and closed his door.

Why, that damned old fraud! Gabe shook his head and dropped his pack on the floor. The man was slick as goose grease, you had to hand him that. Somewhere in his spiel, he'd figured Gabe wasn't any greenhorn and switched his act right in midstream. Tossed out brag and brought sorry into play without even missing a beat. The thing that riled Gabe was that the "honest confession" end of Lucas Harrow's speech was just as phony as the part that came before.

Gabe wasn't sure if he ought to be flat-out irritated or amused. The man couldn't help being what he was. He'd been scamming folks for so long, he wouldn't know honest if he bumped into it in the dark.

Number Three was hotter than an oven and closer to a closet than a room. Near the wall was a straight-back chair mended twice and a dresser with a cracked marble top. The dresser held a basin, a chipped china pitcher, and a towel as thin as Gabe's worst shirt. He didn't have to test the bed. He'd been on a riverboat before and knew a cornhusk mattress by sight.

Gabe took off his duster, dropped his belt and holster on the bed, and peeled off his blue cotton shirt. The water in the pitcher was warm, but he poured the basin full, splashed his face, and ran his fingers through his hair. A smoky mirror was fastened to the wall, but Gabe didn't have to look. He could tell by feeling that the trail dust was gone and he was long overdue for a shave.

Wetting the frayed towel in the basin, he washed his chest and arms as best he could. He'd had a fine bath in a New

Orleans hotel, but that had been three, close to four days ago.

Gabe sat down on the bed. The bad mattress crackled beneath his thighs. He looked at his pack and tried to remember if he had a clean shirt. He vaguely recalled there was one with a tear up the back. If he'd thought, he could've had it sewed up back in New Orleans.

Gabe never thought about clothes until there wasn't anything left to wear. Maybe it isn't torn bad, he thought, and reached down into the pack. When he got up to Jefferson, they'd have some kind of store there. He could look for a shirt and maybe some trousers too. A new pair of socks . . .

The door to Gabe's cabin burst open and slammed hard against the wall, filling the room with harsh light.

Gabe instinctively reached across the bed for his Colt, took a good look at his intruder, and scrambled to his feet.

"Oh my *God*!" the woman cried. Her eyes were bright with fear; someone had savagely ripped her blouse down to her waist. Tangles of raven-black hair clung to the swell of her naked breasts.

"Help me, please!" The woman ran into Gabe's arms, moaned, and fainted against his bare chest.

Gabe had only seen her once before, but he knew who she was. Her husband, or whatever the hell he might be, liked to yell and shake his fists.

This ought to 'bout do it, Gabe thought grimly. If he walks in now, he'll have something to yell about.

CHAPTER TWO

Gabe lifted the woman in his arms and carried her to his bed. Her long hair lay in disarray about her face. Her eyes were closed; her full lips slightly parted. Even unconscious, stretched out limp on her back, the woman's breasts were firm and taut, the nipples dark circles of rose.

Gabe didn't pretend not to look. It would never have crossed his mind to touch a woman who didn't know she was being touched. Still, looking was something else. There was something especially exciting about a half-dressed female helpless and asleep. She looked vulnerable and inviting, wanton and pure—all this at once. It was enough to leave a man with mixed emotions in his head.

Gabe covered the woman with his shirt, turned, and quickly closed and locked the cabin door. It might give people the wrong idea, Gabe thought, but an open door did something worse than that: It gave a short, angry man the chance to walk in at your back. He'd certainly know the woman was gone by now, and he'd very likely want to know where.

Dipping a towel in the pitcher, Gabe pulled a chair up to the bed and gently washed the woman's face. In a moment, she moaned and licked her lips, opened her eyes, and stared at Gabe.

"It's all right," Gabe said. "You're safe."

The woman looked frightened for a second, then seemed to understand where she was.

"Yes, thank you," she said. She looked down at the shirt across her breasts. "Oh dear, I—please, would you turn around a moment? Not that I guess it matters much now."

Gabe stood and looked away. He could hear the woman moving about, the rustle of cloth against her flesh.

"I apologize for . . . barging in on you like this," she said. "I simply couldn't help it. Yours was the first door I saw and I—"

"Ma'am, you don't have to apologize for that. It was pretty clear you needed a place to go."

"Yes. Yes, I did. You may turn around now."

Gabe turned. His shirt swallowed her up. She was a small woman to start with, and the shirt made her look like a child. A child filled out real fine to be sure, but still lost in a grown-up's clothes.

"I'm Corette Clay," the woman said. She held out her hand. "I guess the least I can do is introduce myself."

"Gabe Conrad," Gabe said. "Is there anything I can get you, Miz Clay? The water isn't cold, but it might help some."

Corette shook her head. Her hands twisted nervously in the tail of Gabe's shirt. For the first time, she looked directly at the door.

"My husband is armed," she said calmly. "He is a violent man; I don't suppose I need to tell you that. He carries a small pistol in his vest. If I'm not mistaken, it is a .38-caliber revolver. I don't know the make. I cannot say for certain that he is capable of using this weapon, but I feel you should be aware of this. I am sorry I have put you in a position of danger, Mr. Conrad."

Gabe thought about the stout little man with the big mouth. He was a danger to women and small dogs, all right. And he might just get the nerve to kill you, if you looked the other way long enough, but Gabe didn't figure on doing that.

"I appreciate the warning," Gabe said solemnly. "I'll just be real careful is what I'll do." He listened to the noise of the engine for a moment, then looked at Corette. "I'd guess

your husband's wandering around looking for you right now. Would I be right in saying that?"

"Oh, yes." Corette nodded quickly. "He'll be . . . trying to find me, for sure. He always does."

Always? Gabe thought. Just how often does this sort of thing go on? He wanted to pursue this last remark, but let it go for the moment.

"All right," Gabe said. "I take it for granted you don't much want to be found. That means we'll have to get you somewhere else to stay. I'll go talk to the captain 'bout that, if it's agreeable with you. Lock the door when I go. Don't open up unless you hear me."

Corette stared. "Oh no, I can't do that."

"You can't do what?"

"I can't stay *here*. By myself. And *please* stop calling me Miz Clay. I am—well, I'm in my twenties is where I am. I am not someone's elderly aunt."

Gabe cleared his throat, thinking how she looked beneath the shirt. "Now I never thought that," he said, hoping she didn't take him wrong. "If you won't stay here, I guess you'll have to go with me."

Gabe rummaged through his pack and found the shirt with the tear in the back. He tucked in the tail and strapped the cartridge belt and holster about his waist.

Corette Clay hadn't noticed the Colt before. She blinked at Gabe and looked impressed.

"My, that is . . . somewhat larger than the weapon my husband carries," she said. "Perhaps my warning was unfounded, Mr. Conrad."

"Can't be too careful," Gabe said. "And since you're wearing my best shirt, I'd say you can use my first name, too."

"Gabe—yes, that's a very nice name." Corette forced a smile. "I don't believe I've ever known a Gabe before. From Gabriel, I suppose. God's mightiest angel, who will blow the heavenly trumpet on the Day of Judg—oh, Lord, I just . . . can't *take* this any more!"

Corette's face twisted in pain. "Damn him," she cried. "Damn his rotten soul!"

She burst into tears and buried her face in her hands. Her

body shook in great spasms, and Gabe knew she couldn't stop. He held her gently and let her cry. He wasn't surprised at all. Corette Clay had entered his cabin in a state of hysteria and fear. She had passed out at once; when she woke she was perfectly calm and at ease. It all had to break loose sometime, and Gabe was glad to see it come.

Gabe made certain Corette's husband was nowhere about before he let her out of Number Three. He still didn't like the idea of hauling her all around the ship; the *Cypress Moon* wasn't all that big, and it wouldn't take long to run into everyone aboard.

Keeping his charge close, Gabe checked the wheelhouse atop the boat. The captain wasn't there. The mate looked amused when Gabe asked where he might be.

"It's daylight out, so I reckon he's swillin' coffee somewhere," the mate said. "Sun goes down, he'll switch to gin."

Gabe thanked the man and led Corette down the narrow stairway to the main deck below. The dining room was aft of the noisy boiler. Inside, it was stuffy and hot. Gabe could hear clatter from the galley nearby; the aroma of boiling cabbage was nearly visible in the air.

There were four men in the room. Gabe recognized two of the merchants he'd seen on the deck before. The third man caught Gabe's attention at once. He wore a cheap suit with a broad plaid pattern on a body like a slab of Texas beef. Thick yellow hair framed a face nearly square as a box, heavy brows, a broken nose, and ferret eyes. The man looked briefly at Gabe and let his gaze linger on Corette.

The captain was the fourth man in the room. He sat down his cup and squinted somewhere off to Gabe's right, didn't find anyone there, and shifted slightly to the left.

"I'm Gabe Conrad in Number Three," Gabe said. "This lady's Miz Clay, and she needs a little help."

The captain belched. "What kinda help'd that be?"

Gabe knew he was talking to the captain—but only because of the dirty blue jacket with the tarnished gold buttons. The man inside the coat was a whiskered, cadaverous drunk with red eyes and bad teeth. Gabe figured the mate was wrong:

Gin wasn't just a sundown drink; quite a bit went down the captain's gullet all day.

"I think it'd be a lot better if we talked outside," Gabe said. The other three men were all ears, waiting to see what would happen next. "This doesn't concern anyone but Miz Clay."

"Don't concern me," the captain said, "if I got to do it somewhere else."

The heavyset man beside the captain laughed. Corette started to speak, but Gabe waved her off. He looked at the captain again.

"You got an empty cabin or not?"

"All full up," the captain said.

"You're real sure about that?"

The captain glared. "I ain't used to bein' called a liar, mister."

Gabe decided he strongly doubted the truth of that. He turned to the two merchants.

"You both got your own rooms?"

Both men nodded at Gabe. Gabe pointed to the man on the left. "Now you're bunkin' in with him. You can go get your things out if you like. The lady sure is grateful for your help."

The first merchant stared at Gabe. "I don't *want* to bunk with him."

"I don't blame you," said Gabe.

"I—I won't do it. I'm stayin' where I am!"

"Yes, sir. I believe you will. I think you'll want to do the right thing."

The captain's face clouded. "Who the hell you think you are, mister? You got no business telling my paying passengers what to do!"

"No sir, I don't," Gabe said. "But none of these gentlemen volunteered to help. They're showing bad manners, so I guess *I've* got to do it, too. Miz Clay had an unpleasant experience with Mr. Clay. She needs a cabin of her own. She's asking for help, and I'm asking you gents to pitch in."

The first merchant met Gabe's eyes, didn't see anything he liked, and looked away. "I guess I could—help out if you want. For the lady's sake."

"You've got the right attitude," Gabe said. "Miz Clay here appreciates your kindness."

The man in the plaid suit glanced up narrowly at Gabe. "How come you didn't ask me? I was kind of wonderin' on that."

Gabe let out a breath. He hadn't completely taken his eyes off the heavyset man since he'd entered the room with Corette. His face, his eyes, his whole body spelled trouble. He was a man who couldn't stand to leave well enough alone. He had to stick his nose in, had to see how far he could go. Gabe had spotted the Remington .44 with ivory grips stuck in the big man's belt. He knew a ham-sized hand never wandered too far from the butt.

The thing that concerned Gabe the most was that the man was an outright fool. He was likely half smart when it came to fleecing someone out of fifty cents, but he didn't have much more than oak between his ears. He didn't see the way Gabe stood, the woman behind him to his right, his field of fire clear in every angle of the room.

Gabe's posture was the easy and natural stance of a man who'd learned how to stay alive. The fool didn't see this at all, Gabe knew. He didn't know the rules; he could just as easily do something dangerous and stupid as sneeze. Gabe figured the man had kept himself alive this long by looking like a bear—and not meeting anyone a whole lot brighter than himself.

"You haven't answered me, friend," the man said. "I don't much like to wait."

"Gabe—" Corette's fingers tightened on Gabe's arm.

Gabe shook his head. He saw the man's hand was an inch or so closer to his gun.

"You listen close," Gabe said. "I know what it is you want to do, and I don't care to take the time. Drop your belt on the floor. Get up and step outside. Shuck off that awful-looking suit. Climb up to the wheelhouse and bark like a dog. If you don't, then I'll shoot you in the head."

The man blinked. He wasn't sure he'd heard Gabe right.

"Mister, you're flat crazy if you think I'm goin' to—"

"Make up your mind. Right now."

The man stared at Gabe. He was shaken by what he saw. Gabe's hand wasn't anywhere near the revolver in the crossdraw rig. There was no touch of anger in the pale gray eyes—no anger, no irritation, no emotion of any sort. The heavyset man was a fool, Gabe was right about that. But he was smart enough to see Gabe didn't much care what happened next. Either way was fine with him.

When the man understood this was true, the blood in his veins turned to ice. He couldn't move. The breath stuck in his throat. He looked at Gabe's hands; he couldn't meet his eyes.

"What I said. You might've misunderstood."

"I don't think I did," Gabe said.

"Then I could've made a mistake."

"I guess that's what it was." Gabe looked at the captain and the two other men. No one had budged an inch. "I'd like to get Miz Clay settled in. Maybe we could get these cabins straightened out and have some lunch." Gabe sniffed the air and made a face. "Is that what we're having, what I smell?"

"I am and you ain't," the captain growled. "The cabbage and pigs' feet is mine. The rest of you are getting sliced tomatoes and beef."

"That sounds fair enough to me," Gabe said.

CHAPTER THREE

The captain grudgingly sent a crewman to the Clays' cabin to retrieve Corette's baggage. Luckily, the bad-tempered Mr. Clay was out, wandering about the boat. Gabe helped Corette get settled in, then returned to the dining room for lunch. One of the merchants, a man from St. Louis named Christian, was the only other person about. Christian said the man in the plaid suit was called Holzer. He couldn't recall Holzer's line of work, but Gabe had a fair idea: Holzer's line of work was whatever he could get away with at the time.

Gabe arranged to have a tray sent up to Corette, then walked back out on deck, past the clattering boiler and the high stacks of cargo. The last signs of town life had disappeared some miles back. Settlements and furrowed earth were now replaced by cottonwoods and thick second growth.

Past a sandbar to port, Gabe saw a skeletal tangle of dead trees and brush, a jam twelve or fourteen feet high. These barriers were a constant threat on the river; if a jam blocked the way, all a steamer could do was stop, put out a crew, and scrape the channel free. A jam was always bad news, Gabe knew—but worse than that were the hazards you couldn't see,

like great splintered logs that lay just below the river's surface. If a stern-wheeler hit one of those, she'd rip her belly out, and that'd be the end of that.

Gabe gripped the railing and squinted astern as something the size of a small horse rolled lazily in the boat's muddy wake.

"Alligator gar," said Lucas Harrow, suddenly appearing at Gabe's side. "That one'll likely run to eight feet, maybe four hundred pounds." The old gambler made a face. "Nastiest lookin' fish God ever made. Got lungs and gills both. Can't make up it's mind what the hell it wants to be."

"Isn't too pretty," Gabe said.

Harrow cleared his throat. "Understand you rescued a fair lady this morning. Real knightly thing to do. Sorry I wasn't on hand for the event."

"Don't make a lot out of nothing," Gabe said. He didn't care for the slight glint of amusement in Harrow's eyes. "I helped out some. That's all there was to it."

Harrow shrugged and looked toward the bow, past the trim stacks and high derricks. "I didn't like that Holzer fellow the minute I laid eyes on him. Born scalawag is what he is. Got it written all over his ugly face. Ran into him on the train to Shreveport from Baton Rouge. Came aboard half soused and troubled a couple of ladies till the conductor and some soldiers made him stop. I figure that's the end of that. Then, by God, I'm having a quiet supper by myself last night in Shreveport's finest hotel, and there the bastard is again. Remembered me from the train and near talked me to death. I got up and went to bed. Once more, I thought I was finished with the man."

"I guess you're not," Gabe said.

Harrow looked thoughtfully at his hands. "If I didn't know better, I'd say he was sticking on my tail. Minute I stepped on the *Cypress Moon* there he was, grinning at me like a fool. Heard he mouthed off at you some and backed down. Don't suppose you'd change your mind and shoot the man anyway, would you? Doesn't seem like a lot to ask."

Gabe looked curiously at Harrow. "Any reason why he'd do that?"

"Do what? Follow me, you mean? No reason I can think of." Harrow grinned at Gabe. "Lord God, if every man I'd picked a bone with in my life was to follow me around, there'd be an army back there. They'd clog up the roads. They'd have to carry wagons and supplies."

Harrow tried to laugh the matter off, but Gabe knew he was more concerned than he cared to let on.

"It's not my business," Gabe said, "so you tell me if I'm sticking my nose in or not. This Holzer, he ask a lot of questions? Where you're going, what your business is, things like that?"

"Hardly anything at all," Harrow said. "Mostly, he couldn't get his mind off himself. How well-to-do he was, all the money he'd made."

"Doing what, did he say?"

"Buying cattle is what he said."

Gabe let out a breath. "If that fella ever got closer to a cow than a steak, I'll eat one of those alligator gar."

"I wouldn't advise it," Harrow said.

Gabe spotted a ten-point buck peering at them from the shore, and pointed it out to Harrow. The buck looked wide-eyed, then turned tail and disappeared.

"I'd forget about this Holzer following you around," Gabe said. "A man like that, he gets onto someone serious he's setting them up for a scam. He'll find out everything he can about a man, then figure how to part him from his cash. If he didn't do any prying, he isn't much interested, you can be real sure of that."

Harrow stared at Gabe, then laughed aloud. "This—bumpkin in a mail order suit is going to *cheat* Lucas Harrow? My dear Mr. Conrad. You forget my profession, I fear. Why, if that half-wit had the slightest felonious intent, I would have spotted his efforts a mile away!"

"I reckon you would," Gabe said. He tried not to smile. Harrow had puffed up like a pigeon at the thought that someone might play him for a fool. Gabe hadn't for a moment forgotten that Harrow was a gambler. But he was also a man so pompous and full of himself that a "half-wit" like Holzer might get a little lucky and reel him in. That could never have happened

in Harrow's prime, Gabe was sure—but those days were some years in the past.

"At any rate," Harrow said, fumbling in his coat for a cheroot, "I would say you're quite right. I shall not concern myself with this lout again. If Mr. Holzer should inquire—or anyone else for that matter—my destination is Jefferson, Texas. That should be clear, since there's no place else this aging queen of the river goes." Harrow pointed the tip of his cheroot at Gabe. "You will recall, Mr. Conrad, that I promised you a drink. I am ready to fulfill that obligation now, if you please. A small brandy would not be out of line."

"I'm grateful," Gabe said. "I've got a couple of dozen bad habits, but drinking's not on the list. Suppose you owe me a lemonade, Mr. Harrow, how would that be?"

"I am devastated, of course," Harrow said, "but I will force myself to imbibe alone. Good afternoon, sir. A pleasure to see you, as ever." Harrow touched the brim of his hat and headed forward.

Gabe watched the shoreline a moment, then walked back toward his cabin. No one else was on deck. Gabe wondered where his fellow passengers were keeping themselves. Hopefully, Corette was in her cabin. The captain was likely drunk. Gabe was especially interested in the whereabouts of Holzer and Corette's vile-mannered husband. There were two men aboard a very small vessel who did *not* have warm and friendly feelings toward Gabe Conrad. Neither of the pair were likely the fastest guns in the West, but Gabe knew he'd feel better if he knew where they were. It was the kind of information that helps a man feel more at ease turning corners and walking up narrow flights of stairs.

It was ten degrees hotter in Gabe's cramped cabin, but he decided to give it a try. Stripping off his shirt, he stretched out on the bed and put his hands behind his head. Cabin Number Three was directly above the boiler. The bed constantly shuddered against the floor, and the heat from below added to the fiery air already trapped inside the room.

Just lucky, I guess, Gabe thought. If the boiler explodes, I'll be the first to go. Everybody else'll get burned and crippled up, and I won't have to bother with that.

• • •

Lying on his bed, trying to ignore the heat and noise, Gabe wondered again just what he was doing aboard the *Cypress Moon*, on his way to Jefferson, Texas. There was no one there he knew. It wasn't a place he cared to see. This wasn't the first time he'd wandered off somewhere he'd never been. On the way up from New Orleans, he had reminded himself of that a dozen times. Wandering was simply a way of life, a way he'd chosen some years ago. Being somewhere never did seem as meaningful as where he might go after that.

Only this time was different, Gabe knew. This time it wasn't the same. It didn't *feel* right. Not the way it should. It was not a thing happening to Gabe Conrad, he knew that. The itch at the back of his neck, the sense of something out of place— all of that belonged to his other self, Long Rider. These were feelings that belonged to a boy who had squatted by Lakota fires at night, a boy the shamans had told of *Wakan-tanka*, the Great Spirit, of visions and dreams that led the *oyate-ikse*, the People. Around such fires, Long Rider had learned that Wakan-tanka could protect you or warn you of danger to come. He could send his words to you through the eagle or the wind. He could tell you what would happen through the song of the river, the call of a crow in the woods.

The white man scoffed at the Indians' ways, calling them fanciful superstition, but Gabe had never been tempted to set these strong beliefs of his childhood aside. As far as he could see, the "civilized" world had nothing to offer that was better than the ways of the Lakota.

And, more than once, a dream had come from somewhere to show him a dark and rising river he'd never seen; along with the dream came the feeling in his heart that this was a span of water that he would one day have to cross. Or he would sit by a mountain fire, fully awake, and hear a wild horse in the night. He would get to his feet and search about and find no horse was there.

Sometimes these waking or sleeping dreams seemed to mean nothing at all. Sometimes they were startling visions of events that would change his life. Gabe never knew at the time what such an experience would bring. The moment he had seen

Lucas Harrow, he had been gripped at once by one of these strange feelings. Did it mean anything? Gabe couldn't say. When he was a boy, the shaman of the Lakotas had told him Wakan-tanka, the Great Spirit, always spoke the truth—but that ordinary humans did not always recognize that truth when they saw it.

Gabe sat up straight as someone began to hammer violently on the cabin door. The thin panel shook as if a mule was kicking it with his foot.

"Whatever you want," Gabe called out, "that's not the way to get it. Knock decent, friend, and you might get a decent answer."

At the sound of Gabe's words, the kicking ceased at once. A man began to curse at the top of his lungs. Half a second later, lead ripped through the door, splintering wood and letting daylight in the room.

Gabe hit the floor, grabbing up his Colt on the way. The water pitcher exploded against the wall. The mirror shook, dropped off its nail, and shattered on the floor. Gabe counted six rapid shots, then the unmistakable sound of a hammer snapping down on an empty chamber. Whoever was out there, he didn't have the sense to know his game was all done.

Keeping in a crouch, Gabe grabbed the knob and tore the door aside. Corette's stout and angry husband was standing there gritting his teeth and squeezing off dry shots. Gabe stood, grabbed the man's weapon, and tossed it in the river. Clay looked surprised, as if he'd really expected blasting through the door would put an end to his problems at once. He swung wildly at Gabe, spitting and cursing and turning purple in the face.

Gabe grabbed the back of Clay's collar and the seat of his pants and frog-marched him to the rail. Clay screamed, flailing his arms and legs. Gabe slammed the man's belly down hard on the rail.

"All right, shut your big mouth, you hear?" Gabe said. "Another word out of you and you're swimming with the catfish, mister."

Clay yelled and tried to kick Gabe in the face. Gabe lifted him over the side and let his feet skim the muddy surface of

the river. Clay turned white and shut up. Gabe jerked him back and dumped him on the deck.

"You don't go shootin' at people through doors," Gabe said. He jabbed a finger in Clay's face. "You even *look* like you're carrying a weapon 'round me, and I'll make you eat it. That clear enough for you or not?"

"You—you have interfered with my private affairs," Clay sputtered. "You have no right to poke your nose in my business. You—"

"And you've got no right to go yelling at women and knockin' them around," Gabe said. "It doesn't take much of a man to do that, Mr. Clay. You're a lot bigger than she is, and that's all it takes. Just like I'm a lot bigger than you. You might want to think on that."

"I will *ruin* you, fellow!" Clay shouted. He pulled himself to his feet, backed flat against the wall, and shook his fist. "You don't know who you're fooling with. I will ruin you, wait and see if I don't!"

Gabe looked at the man in disgust. "There isn't any talking to you, is there? A person's got to leave you alone or shoot you dead. I don't guess there's anything in between."

Gabe stalked off toward the bow, leaving Clay cursing at his back. Holzer and one of the merchants were standing by the door of the dining salon. The merchant glanced at Gabe and disappeared. Holzer didn't move. Gabe stopped and glared at the man.

"What the hell *you* looking at? Something you want to talk about with me?"

Holzer stood perfectly still. "I didn't say nothing to you."

Gabe let his eyes rest on the ivory grips of Holzer's pistol. "If I was you," he said evenly, "I wouldn't stick a weapon down my pants. Fellow I used to know had occasion to draw real fast one time. Barrel got hung, and he shot off a real vital part."

Holzer blinked. Gabe turned and left him standing by the door.

I could've hired a 'gator to take me upriver, Gabe thought sourly. Would've sure been a more relaxing trip.

CHAPTER FOUR

Gabe tried to sleep in his cabin, but the sweltering heat kept him fully awake in a pool of his own sweat. Giving up the idea of rest, he rose and dressed again. He was buttoning his shirt when the motion below his feet seemed to change. The deck began to tremble; the engines whined. The *Cypress Moon* shuddered and came nearly to a stop. Seconds later, the engines clattered to life again.

Gabe pulled on his boots and stepped out on the deck. Looking aft, he saw the big paddle wheel was moving slowly, turning just enough to keep the vessel under way. Ahead, fifty yards past the bow, a jam choked the bend of the river. It didn't look bad, nothing like the giant snags that could take a week to clear. Several crewmen were already making their way through the shallows with ropes and axes.

Gabe saw Lucas Harrow and joined him at the bow. Harrow grinned and nodded toward the snag.

"Couple of overgrown logs is all it is," he said. "I've seen a good deal worse."

"I understand they can get pretty big around here," Gabe said.

"The Missouri, now, the Big Muddy herself," Harrow said, paying no attention to Gabe's words. "That was real

riverboating, I'll tell you that. Real riverboating. The Red hasn't ever been much and sure isn't anything to crow about now."

Gabe had to agree. Everyone knew traffic on the Red River was nearly done. Its heyday had come and gone. The Great Raft, debris that had once jammed the Red for close to two hundred miles for more years than anyone could recall, had turned the land upriver into bayou and swamp. Captain Shreve, who gave his name to the port Gabe had just left behind, cleared the Raft and opened the river to trade for a thousand miles upriver. Later, the Raft began to clot up the waters again, and the river backed up clear into Cypress Bayou and let steamers through to Caddo Lake and Jefferson. Jefferson boomed for some years then engineers blasted the Raft once more and all but destroyed steamship traffic to Jefferson—and the wealth that went with it. Now, boats couldn't get upriver until the spring rains, and the way was impassable shortly after that. Gabe was sure that with summer starting up, there might not be more than one or two trips left in the year.

Harrow seemed to guess Gabe's thoughts. "Some years back," he said, "you wouldn't see a captain like the one we've got now on this line. No, sir, you would not. Why, they wouldn't let a man of low character get anywhere near a respectable riverboat. Owners wouldn't stand for it. Passengers wouldn't come aboard. Absolutely not."

"Never saw the Red then," Gabe said. "This is my first trip."

"Mine as well," Harrow said. For a long moment, he was silent. "Didn't ever expect to make the trip I'm making now, I'll tell you that. But damned if I'm not about there."

Harrow looked curiously at Gabe, as if he really didn't see him at all. It seemed to Gabe the old gambler was talking to someone who wasn't there, someone who was miles and years away.

"Don't ever think you've got it all straight in your head," Harrow said. " 'Bout the time you figure you know where you stand, you find out it isn't going to be that way at all."

"It's happened to me once or twice," Gabe said. "I guess everyone gets a surprise now and then."

Gabe half-expected Harrow to respond, but Harrow didn't seem to hear. Then, after a long moment, Harrow came back

Snaketown 25

from wherever he'd been, acting as if nothing unusual had occurred. He launched at once into some fanciful tale about a San Francisco whore.

Gabe waited politely until the man ran down. Then he took his leave and once more climbed the stairs to the hurricane deck.

Evening was on the way, and a slight breeze stirred the hot air. Not enough to do any good, Gabe thought. But maybe just enough to discourage the gnats and mosquitoes for a while.

Someone opened a door on the other side of the deck, and Gabe heard them descending the starboard stairs. He'd nearly reached his quarters when a door opened three cabins down, and Corette Clay stepped out.

"Why, good evening, Mr. Conrad," Corette said. Her smile showed a moment of surprise, but Gabe felt it wasn't real, that she'd been waiting for him to pass.

"You comfortable, ma'am?" Gabe asked.

"Oh yes, I'm fine," Corette said. She had changed into a floral-patterned dress and fixed her hair in a different, more informal manner, Gabe saw. She looked much better than she had before.

Corette's smile faded to show concern. "I, ah . . . understand you had a problem with my husband. I regret that he caused you any trouble. I feel I am to blame."

Gabe looked puzzled. "It wasn't any trouble, and you aren't to blame. Your husband's real good at getting people riled up. He doesn't need a lot of help. He isn't bothering you any, is he?"

"No, no, he's not." Corette shook her head. "I don't think he will, either. William blusters about a great deal, but I do not feel he will care to cross *you* again, sir. I don't believe he has the stomach for that."

You're likely right, Gabe thought. But any man crazy enough to empty his pistol through a door is a man I'm not likely to forget.

"At any rate," Corette went on, "I feel I am perfectly safe for now. I am most grateful to you, Mr. Conrad. I owe you a great deal for your help."

Corette Clay looked at Gabe from under dark and heavy lashes. It was a look that Gabe felt intentionally lingered a second longer than it should. The message seemed bold and quite clear: I owe you, Mr. Conrad, and there might be some way I could pay.

"Well, now don't think anything of it," Gabe said quickly. "Look, Miz Clay—"

"Corette."

"Uh, Corette. It's none of my business, but when we get up to Jefferson, you might want to talk to whoever's the local law. I mean, that's up to you, of course, but I think you know that Mr. Clay isn't about to leave *you* alone. I believe you said this kind of business had happened before. If you've got some family somewhere, you could—"

"*Thank* you, Mr. Conrad." Corette cut him off. "I'm sure I'll be just fine. I will be in no danger from William, and I will not require the help of the law."

"Yeah, well, that's up to you." Gabe didn't know what to say. Corette's smile was perfectly polite, but there was something cold and distant in her eyes. A minute before, the lady had been so damn grateful she was flat-out inviting him to sample her wares. Not that Gabe had any ideas about messing around with a married woman—certainly not one who had a husband who was crazy as a loon—still, what the hell was going on?

"I'm sorry if I said anything out of line," Gabe told her. "That wasn't my intention at all."

"Why, Gabe . . ." Corette looked at him as if she were totally bewildered. "What*ever* made you imagine you could, in any way, be out of line with me? Please perish the thought!"

Corette turned away, walked back into her cabin, and shut the door. Gabe noted her full lower lip was slightly moist, and not from the afternoon heat. Gabe shook his head. Women took a lot of figuring out. It wasn't something a man was up to every day.

The night was stifling hot; heat pressed down like a nearly visible blanket on the river and the dense tangle of trees on either side. If you closed your eyes tight, you wouldn't know

it wasn't day, Gabe thought. All that's missing is the sun.

Not for the first time, Gabe wished he had left the worn denim jacket in his room. A man didn't need an extra layer of anything on this oppressive night. Still, the jacket served a purpose. Earlier, before heading down for supper, he had traded the cross-draw rig around his waist for a belt and holster that looped over his shoulder. This allowed his revolver to hang snugly under his armpit beneath the coat.

Gabe had a reason for switching rigs: To make certain people wonder why he had. It was a simple enough trick, but Gabe knew from experience that it worked. Do something different, and it throws a man off. He figures you wouldn't do something without a reason, so he thinks about that instead of paying attention to what he should.

The shoulder rig worked two ways: It hid a weapon you didn't want someone to see. And, if you left the jacket open just right, you could let someone know that it was there. Gabe had chosen this latter plan for supper. Now, the merchants, the captain, and especially the man named Holzer knew about the shoulder rig. And Gabe had a fair idea word would also reach Corette's husband, William Clay.

Gabe would reveal his shoulder holster if it served a purpose. But there was another side to the rig that a stranger never saw. He had sewn a knife sheath on the underside of the holster. The blade in this sheath hung upside down, the hilt within easy reach. It was a little insurance that had helped Gabe out of a scrape more than once.

Heading aft, Gabe looked high atop the *Cypress Moon* and saw the oil lamps flickering behind colored glass—red for port, and green for starboard. There wasn't much chance another vessel would be coming downstream, but if it did, its pilot couldn't miss the squat stern-wheeler wheezing up the Red.

Pine knots snapped in metal drums at the bow, stern, and amidships along the shallow decks. The drums gave off enough light to keep a passenger from stumbling overboard, but little more than that. Whoever was perched in the wheelhouse, Gabe decided, knew the river by feel instead of sight.

Gabe glanced up at the hurricane deck. The last time he'd checked, a kerosene lamp still glowed behind the porthole of

William Clay's cabin. Corette's porthole was dark. It wasn't all that late, but she might've turned in. What was she wearing, Gabe wondered, lying up there in her room? Some kind of silky thing or what? As hot as it was, she might not have on anything at all.

Gabe let out a breath and brought his thoughts down to earth. Whatever Corette Clay chose to wear, it didn't have a thing to do with him, whether he wanted it to or not. And he was damned if he'd admit the thought had even crossed his mind.

A bright square of light swept the deck as the man called Holzer walked out of the dining salon. Holzer closed the door behind him, shutting out a mix of curses and laughter and the clatter of poker chips.

Gabe watched the man as he lit a smoke and tossed a lucifer into the sluggish current. Holzer leaned on the rail and peered intently across the river, as if there were something there to see past the nearly impenetrable dark. Light from the pine-knot drums threw shadows across the man's broad back and heavily muscled arms. The fellow doesn't have a lot of smarts, Gabe thought, but it wouldn't be wise to get caught in that grizzly bear grip. A man might have trouble getting out.

"Sounds like a real lively game," Gabe said. "Winnin' or losing?"

For an instant, Holzer went stiff. He jerked around to face Gabe, caught himself, and remembered Gabe's rig.

"Winning a couple of hands now and then," Holzer said. "Mostly staying even. Something to sorta pass the time."

Holzer didn't take his eyes off Gabe. The fact that Gabe had spoken didn't please him much at all. Gabe had made him back down. Holzer couldn't forget that. So what did he plan on doing now?

Gabe read Holzer's concern in his eyes. He gave Holzer a grin that didn't help.

"A little game like this can't be all that entertaining," Gabe said.

"I don't guess," Holzer said.

"I've heard about those high-stakes games up in Dodge and Cheyenne. They say you big cattle buyers'll win or lose a fortune at the turn of a card and never bat an eye."

Holzer looked blank. "I don't know what the hell you're—"

Suddenly, Holzer's face flushed with anger. As Gabe had figured, the man had totally forgotten his brag to Lucas Harrow. A man who throws too many stories in the pot can't hardly keep track of the truth.

"I've been in some . . . pretty fancy games, I guess," Holzer said hurriedly. "That was, uh . . . some time back."

"Is that right?" Holzer tried to get by, but Gabe stood his ground. "I bet you've got some good tales. I'd sure like to hear 'em some time."

Holzer glared. "Mister, I got a hand waitin' on me inside. That all right with you?"

Gabe tried to look surprised. "Hell, I'm in the way. I didn't even think about that."

Gabe smiled and stood aside. Holzer brushed past him, and Gabe followed on his heels. Holzer stopped and looked at Gabe with alarm.

"Might just sit in myself," Gabe said.

"Suit yourself," Holzer grumbled and opened the door of the dining salon.

The room was crowded and hot. The air was thick with the smoke from cheap cigars.

"Ah, Mr. Conrad, a hearty good evening to you, sir," Lucas Harrow called out. "Do pull up a chair. Your money's most welcome here."

"Guess I'll just watch for a while," Gabe said.

The captain gave Gabe a sullen glance and looked back at the cards in his hand. One of the merchants nodded hello. Gabe couldn't recall his name.

"Sit over off to the side, you ain't goin' to play," the captain said. "The table's for players; it's not for lookin' on."

"The captain, here, has been having a slight run of ill fortune," Harrow explained, flipping the cards lightly about the table. "Therefore, he is not, for the moment, his charming and gracious self."

"Just deal the damn cards," the captain muttered. "Luck ain't the only problem I got here tonight, not with you dealing."

Harrow stopped. His smile suddenly faded, and his eyes turned to ice. "Just exactly what are you saying, sir? What am I to imply from that remark?"

"Imply whatever the hell you want," the captain growled.

"He don't mean anything at all," Holzer said. "Let's play, damn it."

Gabe watched. He tilted his chair against the wall and kept his eyes on Lucas Harrow's hands. In his time, Gabe figured he'd seen every kind of cheat there was. Men who wore blue glasses to allow them to see phosphorescent marks on the backs of cards. He had seen trimmed-card experts, bottom dealers, and the "feelers" who sandpapered the tips of their fingers so they could sense the smallest needle prick on a pack of cards. At one time or another, he had seen every cheating device you could order from the E. N. Grandine catalog or Will and Finck: Holdout rigs for the sleeves, the vest, and the boot. Gadgets with springs that would allow a man to hide several decks of cards on his person.

Lucas Harrow won—not every hand, he was much too smart for that. He won enough to be a winner, to make a nice profit off the game.

And Gabe saw the captain was right. Harrow was definitely a cheat. It took Gabe half an hour to figure *how* Lucas Harrow was pulling it off. He didn't use any fancy gadgets or employ any ordinary tricks. His method was so simple and devious it was almost impossible to detect. When Harrow dealt, he made a big show of holding the deck close to the table and slipping the cards off low, so it was obvious no one could possibly see them. Only, this was exactly what he *was* doing. He was dealing perfectly straight to Holzer and the merchant, who sat to his left and right—but when he dealt a card to the captain across the table, one corner of each card flipped for the smallest fraction of a second, much too fast for anyone to notice, and too quick to read unless you had a practiced eye. Unless you'd been pulling this trick for fifty years. It wasn't a great advantage in a game with four players, but it would give a man an enormous edge in a high-stakes game with seven or eight around the table. Anytime he was dealing in such a game, he would know the value of seventy-five to eighty percent of

the cards around the table—a very nice edge in any game.

Gabe watched, amused, and more than a little impressed by the old man's talent. He wasn't about to get in this game, but it was interesting to watch.

"Shit, I 'bout as well quit," Holzer grumbled. "I've forgot what a face card's like."

"It's got pitchers on it," the captain said acidly. "Bitches and kings and jacks."

The captain had started winning a few pots and stopped complaining about the cards. Gabe knew Harrow was responsible for the captain's turn of luck. Later, he'd put the screws to the man again.

"What I ought to do," the captain said, "is get a decent job ashore. There isn't nothin' left for a river man. Nothing but leaky tubs like the *Cypress Moon*."

The captain downed another drink and wiped a hand across his grizzled face. Gabe wondered where the old drunk thought he could get a job as good as the one he had. There weren't a lot of positions that required a man to sit around soused all day while someone else did all the work.

"Stay out of the selling trade," the merchant advised, " 'less you fancy losing your shirt. The maker and the buyer get all the money, and you're stuck in the middle with nothing at all."

"Lot of drummers I know get right fat selling doodads ain't worth a dime," Holzer said.

"I suggest you try the trade, sir, before you talk about it."

"Hell, I just might."

"You care for a card," Harrow prompted, "or do I assume you're satisfied?"

"I'm satisfied with two," Holzer said dully, slapping three cards on the table. "These others you can stick wherever you like."

"Patience now, sir," Harrow said.

"Patience, my ass."

"You was whoopin' and hollering a while back," the captain grinned.

"That was when this fella was dealin' something higher than a two."

"Appears to me a man don't like to lose he ought to—*Jesus Christ!*"

Gabe jerked his chair up straight as the door to the salon slammed open like a shot. A dark man with hard, flat features crouched just inside the door, a sawed-off shotgun gripped in both hands. He was naked to the waist. Water dripped from coal-black hair that hung to his shoulders. He swung the weapon about the room, his eyes searching every man there. Gabe wondered if he could make it to the pistol inside his coat. Maybe, but the man would likely get him, too, and Gabe knew who'd lose a tie.

Suddenly, Lucas Harrow moved, reaching for something in his vest.

"No, *don't!*" Gabe cried out.

The shotgun moved in a blur, twin barrels looking for Gabe's belly. Harrow came out of his chair; Gabe hit the floor, clawing for his weapon, as Harrow threw himself at the intruder. The shotgun roared once and then again, the sound loud and terrible within the small room.

Lucas Harrow came apart; blood and bone spattered the walls, and bits of torn flesh struck Gabe in the chest. Gabe came to his feet, stumbling over the ragged upper half of Lucas Harrow, firing the Colt at a suddenly empty room.

Someone shouted at his back—Gabe couldn't tell who. He ran through the door keeping low, stopped, and blinked against the night. A sound reached him above the clatter of the engines; jerking to his right he saw the man leap off the deck into the dark. Gabe snapped off two quick shots, but knew he hadn't hit a thing. The killer was gone, lost in the vessel's wake.

My God, the man's fast, Gabe thought. He was there in the room, and then he wasn't there at all.

Gabe felt a touch of cold at the base of his spine. If the old man hadn't played the fool, that would have been him in there, cut clean in two. The thought came to him then that he was sorry Lucas Harrow was dead, and glad that Gabe Conrad was alive. It might not be a real proper thought at the time, but he knew that it was true.

CHAPTER FIVE

No one aboard the *Cypress Moon* got much sleep for the rest of the night. Men wandered about the decks, telling each other what had happened, living the moment a dozen times, as if telling the story might assure them they were fine, that it was someone else who was stretched out cold under canvas in the stern.

Gabe stayed away from all the talk. He didn't need anyone to tell him he was lucky to be alive. The scene was burned into his memory like a brand. Lucas Harrow, stepping into the line of fire, taking the deadly twin barrels for him. *Why*, though? Why would the old gambler give his life for a man he hardly knew? Gabe could find no answer to that.

He thought once more about the killer. Like the moment of Harrow's death, it was an image he'd never forget. Broad, Indian features and hard, black eyes. A half-breed, Gabe had guessed at the time, and learned soon enough he was right. The captain had seen his face on a poster in Jefferson, Shreveport, and other towns along the river. No one knew his real name, but they called him Caddo Jack. Over the past year and a half, he had robbed and killed travelers on the roads. Twice, he had walked boldly into Jefferson itself, murdering a storekeeper in

broad daylight and, the next night, slitting a woman's throat while she slept. Now, he had climbed aboard the *Cypress Moon* and shot Lucas Harrow in half.

And why had he done that? Gabe wondered. All his other killings had seemingly been for profit, and he hadn't gained a dime from the *Cypress Moon*. It didn't make a lot of sense, Gabe knew. Still, coldblooded killers weren't the most rational people in the world. There was no use trying to figure what made them tick.

With the first pale light of dawn, the cook brought cold fried eggs, stale toast, and strong coffee from the galley onto the open decks. No one cared to eat, but the coffee pot was emptied several times. The dining salon was closed for the trip. Even after Harrow's body had been removed, the room looked as if someone had lobbed an artillery shell into a butcher shop.

Gabe found the captain leaning over the starboard rail. The events of the night before had sobered him fast, but he was catching up as quickly as he could.

" 'Bout an hour out of Jefferson," he said, giving Gabe a bleary look. "Won't be too soon for me. I don't need no corpse on my boat, I'll tell you that."

Lucas Harrow isn't enjoying the trip either, Gabe thought, but kept his comments to himself.

"This Caddo Jack," Gabe said, "he ever do anything like this before? I figure you'd know if he did."

"You're right, I would. And no he ain't." The captain shook his head. "First time he's pulled a stunt like this."

"Why do you think he did it, then?"

The captain gave Gabe a curious look. "Shit, you was there. Bastard tried to hold up a poker game. Now *that's* been done before."

"Doesn't make sense," Gabe said. "He didn't know we'd be having a game. No way in the world he could have figured on that."

"So what?" The captain spat over the rail. "He came aboard 'cause he heard about the good food I serve. Maybe he just had an itch to kill and rob everyone. How the hell do I know?"

Gabe had to admit the man was right. No one would likely

ever know what had gone through the Indian's head. Maybe he'd never been on a riverboat before. Maybe he didn't have anything else to do.

A picture of Lucas Harrow kept forming in Gabe's head. The old man was dead, and for no good reason at all.

"Harrow's things," Gabe said. "I'd like to have a look at them, captain, if it's all the same to you."

"What for?" The captain looked narrowly at Gabe.

"Just want to see if he's got family somewhere. If there's anything he had with an address on it."

"Don't guess it'll do any harm," the captain said. "You'll have to give everything back. That's the company rules."

"All I want's a name. Something that shows where he's from."

The captain nodded, left for a moment, and came back with a small canvas sack.

"Everything's listed proper. That's the rules. He had a gold watch, a hundred and forty-two dollars and some change, a wallet, a pen knife, and a letter. That's it."

"I'd like to see the wallet and the letter," Gabe said, wondering how much Harrow had been carrying before the captain made his inventory.

The captain picked the two items from his sack. The letter was badly stained with blood.

"Thanks," Gabe said, "I'll get these things back to you."

"Make damn sure you do," the captain said.

Gabe set the letter aside and searched through Harrow's wallet. There was half of a used railway ticket, a card from a Houston saloon, and a receipt from a Shreveport hotel. Gabe read the receipt and frowned. The name on the receipt read Joshua Porter—not Lucas Harrow. Gabe picked up the letter. The address on the envelope was too blurred to read. The letter inside read:

My Dear Brother Joshua,
  You and I have been apart for too long. Everything that has gone before has been forgotten and belongs to years past. Both of us are growing older, and it would

give me great pleasure to see you. I mean no disrespect, Joshua, but I have no way of knowing your financial situation at the moment. Therefore, I am enclosing a draft for $100.00. I hope you will accept my invitation to come and stay with me in Jefferson, Texas, as soon as possible.

>Your Loving Brother,
>Robert L. Porter,
>Jefferson, Texas

Gabe put down the letter. From the hotel receipt and the letter, it was clear that Joshua Porter was likely Harrow's real name. Not too unusual, Gabe thought, using another name. A lot of men had good reason to pick another name once or twice in their lives. A man in Harrow's profession had probably gone through a few dozen.

He was going home, Gabe thought, going back to see his family, and he damn near made it. He recalled the man's words, when they had stood at the bow and watched the crew clearing away a snag.

"Didn't ever expect to make the trip I'm making now, I'll tell you that. But damned if I'm not about there..."

Harrow had spoken these words and stared off miles and years beyond the river. And Gabe knew he wouldn't have to worry about finding the man's family. They were waiting for him a few miles ahead.

A sudden noise outside shattered Gabe Conrad's thoughts. He came quickly to his feet and opened the door. On the deck down below, William Clay was screaming at his wife, shaking his fist before her face. Corette was pressed back against the rail, her eyes wide with fright.

Gabe cursed under his breath and took the stairs three at a time. Stalking up behind Clay, he grabbed the man's collar and jerked him away from Corette.

"I've about had enough of you, mister," Gabe said. "This hasn't been a real pleasant trip, and your presence hasn't helped a damn bit."

"Take your hands off me," Clay sputtered. "By God, I'll have your hide!"

Snaketown 37

"We'll talk about that some time," Gabe said. "I don't much care to discuss it now."

Gabe grabbed the man by the collar and the seat of his pants and heaved him overboard. William Clay squealed like a pig and hit the dirty water hard. Gabe waited till he surfaced, cursing and spitting silt, then turned to Corette.

"Can your husband swim, ma'am? I guess I should've asked."

Corette stared at Gabe. Her expression turned from disbelief to fury, and she slapped him hard across the face.

"You—you *ruffian*," she cried, "just who do you th-think you are! Why don't you mind your own business, you big lout!"

Corette turned and stomped off toward the stern, shouting hysterically to her husband. William Clay had made it to the shallows. He stood on a sandbar, shaking himself like a large wet dog.

Gabe looked after Corette and shook his head. Now what kind of gratitude was that? A man tries to do the right thing and gets hit. His face still smarted from the blow, and he was glad Corette hadn't doubled up her fist. For a fairly small lady, she packed a real punch.

The captain walked up and looked sadly at Gabe. "I kinda wish you hadn't done that. Now I'll have to stop the damn boat."

"Like hell you will," Gabe said. He poked a finger in the captain's chest. "It's either him or me on board, and I don't intend to get off."

The captain scratched his chin. "I expect you'll get in trouble over this. Man like that don't take too kindly to being tossed into the Red."

"Guess I'll manage," Gabe said. "I been in trouble before."

CHAPTER SIX

The *Cypress Moon* wheezed into the docks at Jefferson, Texas, at half past ten. The cloudless sky was the color of ash, and the sun already scorched the earth.

Gabe Conrad stood in the bow and watched the roustabouts swarm aboard the boat to start hauling the cargo ashore. Most of the workers were black, but a few were of Indian blood. Gabe felt a catch in his throat when he saw these men with their long, black hair and burnished copper flesh. Once, they would have been proud warriors, but now they eked out a miserable living working for the whites. Gabe had seen this sight many times, and it never failed to fill him with anger and regret.

The shore was lined with brick warehouses, many of them clearly empty now, hollow reminders of Jefferson's better days. In years past, a dozen river steamers would have crowded close together at the town's wharves. Now, only the *Cypress Moon* and one other shabby boat were nosed into the shore.

The moment the *Cypress Moon* touched the dock, her passengers were ready to go ashore. No one wanted to stay aboard a second longer than they had to; no one had pleasant memories of their short trip up the Red.

Snaketown

The captain put a stop to this exodus at once. "You'll just have to wait," he said. "I've sent a man runnin' into town to get the law. We got a corpse on board, and that's the company rule. Isn't anyone leaving till we've taken care of that."

The passengers protested, but the captain wouldn't budge. The merchants began to argue among themselves. Gabe saw the man named Holzer brooding off by himself. Corette Clay wouldn't look at him at all.

A few moments later, the captain's crewman appeared on the wharf. At his heels was a tall, rawboned man wearing faded cotton trousers, a clean white shirt, and a broad-brimmed straw hat. His face seemed etched from hard rock, and Gabe could see a lawman's badge shining on his chest.

As soon as the tall man came aboard, the captain took him off to the side. The captain talked, and the lawman listened. Finally, the captain handed the man the letter Gabe had read. The lawman examined the bloodstained paper. A startled expression touched his features, and he sent the captain's crewman scurrying back along the wharves toward town. As soon as the crewman was gone, the lawman stalked up to the passengers and looked them over, taking everyone in with his hard blue eyes.

"I'm Jake Harper," he announced, "sheriff of Jefferson, Texas. You all come on back here with me, if you will. I'll get you off this boat as quick as I can."

"Listen, sheriff, I've got things to do," Holzer said. "I haven't got time to waste here."

Sheriff Harper ignored him. He walked back to the stern, bent down, and peered under the canvas at Lucas Harrow's corpse. He studied the cold features a moment then stood.

"The captain here's told me what happened. A half-breed come aboard and shot this feller in half. Anyone got something to add to that?"

No one said a word. Harper's eyes flicked about the circle and landed on Gabe.

"What about you? Understand you was friendly with this man."

"Don't guess I saw anything the rest of 'em didn't see," Gabe said.

"Is that right?"

"That's what I just said, sheriff."

Harper nodded and looked away. "I got a wanted poster on this Caddo Jack. I'd like everyone here to stop by my office in town and take a look."

"It was him, all right," the captain said. "Isn't any doubt about that."

Harper didn't seem to hear. He walked up close to Gabe. "Captain says you went and tossed a man overboard. Is that right?"

"Near as I recall, that's what I did," Gabe said.

"Near as you recall?"

"Uh-huh."

"What for?"

"Seemed like the right thing to do."

Harper gave Gabe a nasty grin. "You reckon I got one of them posters with your picture on it? You think I ought to have a look?"

Gabe looked as thoughtful as he could. "Seems to me I threw a lady in a stock pond once, but that was some time ago. She didn't seem to mind."

One of the merchants laughed, but Harper stilled him with a glance.

"You ought to put him in jail," Corette said. "That's what you ought to do!"

"She's the fella's wife," the captain said.

Sheriff Harper took off his hat, revealing a shock of yellow hair. "That right, ma'am? Fella got thrown in the Red belong to you?"

"I am Mrs. William Clay, yes," Corette said stiffly.

"You want to file a charge on this man?"

"I—yes, I mean—" Corette glanced quickly at Gabe and looked away. "I guess I should, shouldn't I? I mean, he had no *right* doing a thing like that. He deliberately—"

Corette stopped. In an instant, her expression turned from anger and confusion to relief.

"Oh, Elaine," she cried out, "I'm *so* glad you're here!"

Corette swept past Gabe and the others. Gabe turned and saw her throw herself into the arms of another woman.

A gaunt, middle-aged man in a well-tailored, brown, worsted suit stood just behind the woman. He might as well have been invisible, for Gabe hardly noticed he was there. The woman who had gathered in Corette was a breathtaking beauty, and Gabe had seen more than a few. Dark hair the color of smoke tumbled over her bare shoulders. The dress that hid the swell of her breasts matched startling green eyes. She comforted Corette, touching her gently on the back, but the green eyes reached out and found Gabe.

Gabe felt the heat of her glance. She was a tall girl, nearly as tall as Gabe himself, and built to fill her oversized frame. Her skin was milk and honey; her nose was perfectly straight, except for a rebellious tip at the end; and her lips were full and red.

Sheriff Jake Harper caught the woman's bold appraisal of Gabe Conrad and didn't seem to like it at all. He stepped in front of Gabe and faced the man in the brown suit.

"I'm real sorry to get you down here like this, Mr. Porter," Harper said, "but I guess I got some real bad news."

Porter seemed puzzled. "What's the meaning of this, Jake? What the hell are you talking about?"

Harper cleared his throat. "It's . . . your brother, sir. He's been killed. We think it was Caddo Jack."

Porter's face turned white, and Gabe thought the man might choke. "Nonsense," Porter blurted, "that's impossible!" He stared at the canvas-covered body in the stern. "I haven't even *heard* from my brother in thirty years!"

Harper gave Porter a curious look. "Ah, you weren't expecting him then, Mr. Porter?"

"Of course I wasn't expecting him. Don't know where he is, and don't care to, either!"

"Mr. Porter—"

"Are you plain deaf or what, Jake?" Porter glared at Harper. "For God's sake, man, I'll put an end to this foolishness right now."

Porter pushed roughly past the sheriff and squatted down over the covered corpse.

"Father—" The woman reached out to stop him, but Porter didn't hear. He lifted up the canvas and peered at the dead and

bloodless features. For a moment, he showed no reaction at all. Then, he jerked back so swiftly he nearly fell.

"*Jesus. . . . Oh, Jesus God!*" he moaned. "Jesus God, it's him!"

Porter's daughter went quickly to her father's side. She bent down and put an arm around his shoulder and helped him up.

"It's him," Porter muttered again to himself. "It's Josh. . . . It's Josh, Elaine, it's him. . . ."

"Mr. Porter—" Sheriff Harper looked as if he wanted to sink right into the deck, as if he might be blamed for all this. "Sir, I'm real sorry, but I got to do this official, you know? You've identified the, uh, remains, as your brother, Mr. Joshua Porter, is that right?"

Porter didn't answer. Elaine looked at Harper. "Consider it official, Jake, all right? I'll talk to you later."

Harper nodded, and Elaine led her father back to the bow. Corette Clay followed them both, looking thoroughly confused.

Harper frowned at Gabe. "*You* don't go anywhere out of town, you understand?" He poked a finger at Gabe. "I got to send a boat down to pick up that feller you tossed in the drink. After that, you and me are going to talk."

"I won't be hard to find," Gabe said.

"I'm countin' on that," Harper said, then stalked away.

Gabe watched him go. He walked forward then and followed the two women and the man with his eyes until they climbed into a carriage at the dock. Porter's daughter Elaine, now that was some woman, one he sure hoped to see again. Harper didn't have to worry too much—even if Gabe had figured on leaving town, he'd stay around a while to see her.

Harper directed the roustabouts back to the stern to get Joshua Porter's corpse, the man Gabe had known as Lucas Harrow. Gabe leaned against the railing and watched them lift the stiffened form.

Harrow thought his brother wanted him home, Gabe thought, only his brother didn't know anything about it. There was no way Porter could have shown such emotion if the feelings weren't real. So who had invited Harrow to Jefferson, Texas?

Snaketown 43

Gabe wondered what Robert Porter would think when Sheriff Harper got around to showing him the letter.

Gabe let out a breath. He had a head full of questions and no answers to go with them. So what? he thought. Isn't anything new about that.

CHAPTER SEVEN

Gabe slung his pack over his shoulder and walked from the wharves toward town. Jefferson was surrounded by tall pine trees and thick-boled oaks. Rain hadn't touched the *Cypress Moon* on the trip upriver, but storms had clearly swept through the town. Visible clouds of steam heat rose up from the muddy streets. Gabe stayed to the narrow board sidewalks when he could. A wagonload of timber splashed by through the mire. Mud splattered several morning shoppers, but the black teamsters driving the rig only grinned and whipped their mules into a faster pace.

Gabe had heard of the Excelsior Hotel. People all over Texas talked about its fine food and rich, stylish appearance. With Jefferson on the decline, he had half expected the hotel to be somewhat less than elegant now, but apparently the Excelsior was holding its own. The lobby was as grand as any he'd ever seen in St. Louis or San Francisco. There was a magnificent chandelier that would have looked right at home in any palace, sofas of patterned silk, gilt mirrors on every wall, and fine carpets covering the polished hardwood floors.

Gabe signed in and ordered up a hot bath.

"How long will you be staying in Jefferson, sir?" the clerk wanted to know.

"Sorta depends," Gabe said.

"Well, that's fine. You're welcome as long as you like."

Before Gabe could start up the stairs, the clerk pointed out the old register on display and opened it to a well-thumbed page.

"Guess you know about Jefferson," the clerk said. "Lot of history here."

"I reckon there is," Gabe said, anxious to get up to his room and get a bath.

"Right here," the man pointed, "this is where the famous millionaire Jay Gould signed in. Come to Jefferson and told the townfathers he'd like to run the T & P through town. Well, they turned him down flat. Said: 'We've got steamboats here, what do we need a railroad for?' Old Gould signed the register—see his name? January 2, 1872. Third name from the top. Drew a flying jaybird and wrote down 'Gould.' And at the bottom of the page, he wrote, 'End of Jefferson, Texas.' Told us grass'd be growing in the streets and bats would nest in the churches."

The clerk shook his head and grinned. "Damn near right he was, too. Hasn't happened yet, but it will."

"Still looks like a right fine town," Gabe said politely.

"Not what it used to be, though. No, sir. We'll never see those days again."

Gabe found his room was a miniature copy of the lobby. There were fine mirrors and carpets, marble-top tables, a tall armoire, and a cherry-wood bed. When the buckets of hot water arrived, he soaked a good hour, leaving the tub as dark as the Red River itself. Dressed again, he headed for the dining room downstairs and feasted on cold roast beef and tomatoes, new potatoes, greens, and apple pie. A waiter brought him a copy of the *Jefferson Jimplecute*, but Gabe found little of interest to read.

He was finishing his coffee and pie when he looked up and saw Sheriff Jake Harper crossing the broad dining room toward his table.

"Mind if I join you?" Harper said. Without waiting for an answer, he pulled out a chair and sat.

"You ought to try some of this pie," Gabe said. "Best I ever had."

Harper shook his head. He rested his elbows on the table and looked at Gabe.

"You might be in a little trouble, mister," Harper said flatly. "I might be haulin' you off to jail this afternoon."

"Glad I went ahead and had dinner," Gabe said. "Doubt if you can match the food here."

Harper's expression didn't change. If he was annoyed, he was determined not to let himself show it. "Sent a couple of boys down to pick up Mr. William Clay. He's not real happy with you."

"That man's not real happy with anyone, far as I can see," Gabe said.

"What you ought to do when you're thinking 'bout tossing someone in the river is first find out who they are. That'd be a good idea."

"I know who he is."

"No, you don't," Harper said. "What he is, is president of the biggest bank in St. Louis, Missouri. He's a real important man over there. His wife, Mrs. Corette Clay, is first cousin to Miss Elaine Porter, who's the daughter of Mr. Robert L. Porter, president of *our* biggest bank."

Gabe looked up. "And the brother of Josh Porter, who got himself shot in half on the *Cypress Moon*. How do you reckon Mr. Porter didn't know his brother was coming, Sheriff, when Josh had a letter inviting him here? I haven't been able to figure that."

"I don't see how that's any of your concern, do you? I'm damned if I do." For the first time, Harper's face betrayed his irritation.

"You aren't even curious?" Gabe said.

"It's none of my business, either. I don't pry into Mr. Porter's affairs."

Gabe finished off his pie and signaled the waiter for more coffee. "Seems kind of peculiar," he said. "If Mr. Porter didn't write that letter, who did? You get around to showing it to him yet?"

"What the hell difference does it make who wrote the damn

letter?" Harper said shortly. "A man got murdered by that stinkin' half-breed. *That's* my concern, not who's writing letters and who's not."

Gabe sat up straight and looked Harper in the eye. "It makes a difference to me. That would've been me cut in half if Lucas Harrow or Josh or whoever he was hadn't gone after this Caddo Jack. That makes me feel obligated, Sheriff."

"Yeah, all right, I can understand that," Harper admitted. "But isn't much you can do about it now." Harper stopped suddenly and squinted at Gabe. "You want to tell me what you're thinking, mister? It better not be what I *think's* going through your head."

"Don't know as I'm thinking on anything at all," Gabe said.

"The hell you're not." Harper gripped the table and leaned in toward Gabe. "I'll tell you just once. Caddo Jack's the law's business, not yours. If you're figuring on interfering with the law, I'd take it real personal. That plain enough?"

"Plain enough, Sheriff."

"Good. I'm sure glad to hear it." Harper stood and hitched up his belt. "Enjoy that pie. Any luck at all, you'll be dinin' on stale bread and water for breakfast."

Harper walked off, stomping heavily enough to rattle crystal on his way through the Excelsior's dining room.

There's a man carrying a chip on his shoulder, Gabe thought. Only Jake Harper's chip is the size of a yellow pine log. Gabe wondered if very many men had tried to knock it off. Harper was as lean as a post, but it would be a big mistake to overlook the wiry muscle bunched up like cords of rope beneath his shirt. The man could take care of himself and likely didn't need to draw his big Colt .45 a whole lot.

Another thought about Jake Harper came immediately to mind. Gabe clearly recalled the look in the sheriff's eyes when Elaine Porter came aboard the *Cypress Moon*, and Harper caught her sizing up a man she'd never seen. If Harper could have shot me on the spot, Gabe thought, he'd be a happy man. Whether that tall, green-eyed lady knew it or not, Harper considered her his private preserve.

Gabe paid his bill and walked out into the humid streets

of Jefferson. Hell, if he wasn't in jail by sundown, he'd be surprised. Locking him up would give Harper more pleasure than a whole year of birthdays with Christmas thrown in.

Gabe stopped at a store several blocks from the Excelsior Hotel and bought a box of cartridges, dried beef, a bag of beans, and a sack of flour. He picked out several other items, including a brand new shirt, and had them sent over to his room.

Jefferson seemed busy enough. There were horses, carriages, and wagons on the streets, but it was clear the town's affluence was a thing of the past. There were plenty of boarded up shops; white herons nested in the windows of warehouses that had once been piled to the rafters with goods.

Gabe walked past the Excelsior again and the big stone Federal Building. At Walnut and Austin he saw the imposing face of the Planter's Bank and wondered if it belonged to Robert Porter. Maybe, or maybe not. At any rate, the building looked solid enough, as if it intended to be around for some time.

After walking only a few blocks, Gabe found himself at the edge of town. Behind him lay the everyday sounds of civilization. Ahead was an almost impenetrable thicket of trees and tangled brush. Other people had been this way before, and Gabe followed a rough pathway past great live oaks and patches of green fern. Without warning, the river appeared through the trees. Gabe found a fallen log and sat. The wilderness around him had gone silent at his approach, but in a moment or two, familiar sounds began to fill the humid afternoon. Birds cried out, and something moved through the brush nearby. A cottonmouth slid off the bank and curled its way out across the water.

Gabe was glad for the chance to be alone. He didn't shun the company of other men, but he didn't need them, either. Men of the Lakota cherished their friends and family, but they treasured their solitude as well. They did not feel alone in the woods or on the vast Western plains. To them, the whole world was alive. They knew they were a part of the waters and the sky; wherever they might be, there was always other life

about. The wolf, the bear, the eagle up above, the grass below, all were part of the living earth.

When he entered the world of the whites as a young man, Gabe was still very much Long Rider, and he was dismayed to learn the whites felt they were entirely alone if there was not another man or woman about. They firmly believed that they and they alone were the only significant inhabitants of the earth and that all other life had somehow been placed there for their enjoyment.

Gabe did not understand this way of thinking then, and he could not understand it now. All his adult life he had watched the white man take what he wanted and waste half of that. If a man needed a house, he would fell enough timber for three and leave the rest to rot. He would shoot a hundred geese and eat two.

Whenever such thoughts crossed his mind, he felt a sudden surge of anger, sorrow, and regret. Right up to the end, the copper-skinned inhabitants of the great American continent had believed there had to be an end to the white man's advance, that he would, eventually, feel he had enough and stop. That he would come to understand that he could not take everything for himself. Too late, the Indian peoples learned that there would never be enough. The white man stopped taking when he reached the great ocean to the west, when he ran out of land, and there was nothing more to take.

If they had found some way to steal all the salt water, then they would have, Gabe thought grimly. It's a wonder they didn't bottle it and make the Indians buy it back.

A sound that didn't belong cut into Gabe's thoughts. He turned on his log and listened, his hand near the Colt, his eyes on the pathway through the woods.

A flash of green satin appeared through the trees; a few seconds later, Elaine Porter walked toward him down the path.

Gabe stood at once, surprised by the girl's appearance there and startled again by her beauty.

"I hope you don't mind the intrusion," Elaine said. "I saw you go into the woods and thought we might talk for a while."

By God, Gabe thought, I don't much care why you came, girl, just as long as you did.

CHAPTER EIGHT

"I'm . . . pleased you want to talk," Gabe said, trying to find the right words. "I mean, I'm real glad you came."

Elaine held out her hand. "I'm Elaine Porter. We haven't been properly introduced, but I know who you are. I expect you know who I am, too."

"Yes, ma'am, I do," Gabe said.

Elaine laughed. "I think Elaine will be just fine. If I can call you Gabe."

"Gabe'll be good."

"Well, I guess we've got all the introducing part settled."

"I guess we do."

Elaine smiled and let herself down gracefully on the log beside Gabe. Gabe tried to keep his eyes off her soft bare shoulders and the plunging vee of her neckline, but it was hard to look anywhere else. Elaine seemed to know what he was doing and didn't blush.

"Gabe, I'll get right to it so you won't keep wondering why I'm here," Elaine said. "I know what you intend to do. I know you're going after Caddo Jack."

Gabe squinted thoughtfully at the girl. "What makes you think that? Seeing as how we've never talked before."

"Well, you practically told Jake Harper that you were."

"And Harper told you."

Elaine shrugged and looked out at the river. "Jake Harper tells me everything he knows. He . . . fancies that we have some kind of a . . . relationship."

"And do you?"

"That wouldn't be of any concern to you, now would it?"

"You're right about that."

"Well, is it true? Are you going after Caddo Jack?"

"It's something I've got to do," Gabe said.

Hearing himself voice his thoughts to the girl made Gabe feel strangely ill at ease. Of course he was going after Lucas Harrow's killer. It had never occurred to him to do anything else. It wasn't something you *decided* to do, any more than you decided to breathe. It was true he had told Jake Harper, and he'd gone and bought himself some supplies. Still, he considered these less than conscious acts; he'd never really expanded his intentions to himself until now.

Gabe knew he couldn't explain that to Elaine or to anyone else. The Oglala had taught him there were things a man did that required no decision or thought of any kind. Going after a man who killed your friend was a matter of honor. It was something you simply did. The part of Gabe that belonged to Long Rider knew that and didn't have to think about it twice.

"I guess I talk too much," Gabe said finally. "It didn't take long for the word to get around."

"This is a very small town," Elaine said. "There aren't a lot of secrets that stay secret long."

Elaine picked up a willow twig and started peeling off the green skin. "If you stay in Jefferson more than a day or two, you'll hear another secret, Gabe. Everybody here knows it, so you might as well hear it from me. My father settled here some twenty-five years ago. He had some money when he got here, and he made a lot more after that. You couldn't tell it now, but he must have been a pretty headstrong young man."

Elaine paused. "My mother's name was Lil. Father found her selling tomatoes and onions by the river. She was way below his station, as they say. She came from poor stock, somewhere down around Sour Lake. But she was a real beauty,

and Father had to have her. He generally gets everything he wants. He married her and scandalized the town. No one ever said a word to his face, of course. When you're rich, people smile at you and talk behind your back.

"My mother was fifteen years younger than my father. He was thirty-one, and she was sixteen. He thought he could tame her, but she was used to running wild.

"He . . . Father whipped her and tried to keep her home." Elaine turned away. "I remember some of that. Mother screaming and cursing my father, and Father hitting her all the harder. I was about six, but I remember it clear. She left him for good when I was ten. Father just about went crazy. He took his meanness out on me. He wasn't so crazy he didn't know that was wrong, and he sent me off to school back East. I stayed away till I was twenty. That was nearly six years ago."

Elaine looked at Gabe, and Gabe saw the lovely green eyes fill with tears. He wanted to reach out and hold her, take her in his arms, but didn't think she'd take too kindly to that.

"I hated my father for a long time," Elaine went on. "I've just about gotten over that. Maybe he had reason to lose control. I guess a lot of men do. He shouldn't have whipped her, though. He shouldn't have ever done that."

Gabe looked down at his hands. "I can see you had some problems growing up, all right. I'm real sorry about that. A person needs a mother and a father both to help 'em turn out the way they should."

Gabe faced Elaine. "You'll pardon me for saying this, but I guess I don't see why you're telling all this to me. You and your family aren't any of my business, Elaine."

"You're quite right," Elaine said. "It isn't your concern. I told you this so you'd know. It's the part of our . . . sordid family history you won't hear from my father."

Gabe frowned, and Elaine saw the question in his eyes. She stood and brushed away the bits of grass and leaves that clung to her skirts.

"My father wants to talk with you," she explained. "Supper at the Excelsior at eight, if that's all right with you."

Gabe stood. "I'll be glad to do it, but I don't see why he'd want to talk to me."

Elaine showed him a patient smile. "I told you there were few secrets in this town, Gabe. Jake Harper told me about his talk with you but he told my father first. Everyone in Jefferson does that. Bankers have a way of instilling a certain kind of loyalty in people. I'm sure you know that."

"I haven't had a lot of dealings with bankers," Gabe said.

"Then count yourself lucky." Elaine grinned. "If supper's all right, I'll tell Father. Eight, at your hotel."

"Mind if I ask you something?"

"Please do."

"Was this your father's idea or yours?"

"Why his, of course. My goodness, why would *I* invite you to supper, Mr. Conrad? That wouldn't be proper at all."

Elaine's eyes widened with such innocence that Gabe couldn't hold back a grin.

Elaine blushed. "Well, it is mostly his idea. Really. I will say I encouraged him a little."

"I'm glad that you did," Gabe said. He held her gaze a long moment. Elaine finally cleared her throat and nervously touched the vee of her gown.

"Incidentally," she said, "I think I should tell you in all honesty that I approve of what you did to William Clay. He is a man I cannot respect at all. He is an abuser of women, and I have seen quite enough of that in my life."

"Why doesn't his wife leave him?" Gabe asked. "A woman doesn't have to put up with that."

"Oh, but a woman does," Elaine said gravely. "If she wants to survive, she does. Do you think William Clay would allow her to leave? And if by chance she did, what would she do? He would leave her penniless, you can bet on that."

Elaine sighed. "Still, I must agree with you, Gabe. *I* would not put up with the man for an instant. But I fear cousin Corette is one of those women who . . . somehow delight in being used. She was like that even as a child. I can't say why, but she was."

"Maybe she went through some of the same kind of treatment you did," Gabe suggested.

"I—I never considered that. Quite possibly you are right. I didn't know her family all that well. Still . . ."

Elaine shook the thought aside. "We didn't expect William and Corette until next week sometime. I'm quite glad she's here. Maybe I can talk some sense into her while Father and William talk about all the money they've made."

"Well, I won't apologize to him," Gabe said, "but tell your cousin I'm sorry if I caused her any worry. I thought I was helping out, but she didn't much see it that way."

"Oh, she's not angry with you any longer, I assure you. She stays so furious at William, she doesn't have time to be mad at anyone else."

Elaine looked mischievously at Gabe. "William, now, there's a man who wants your hide. Lord, I wish you could have seen him when they brought him upriver and deposited him at our house. He was covered with bug bites and scratches, and I *swear* steam was coming out of his ears. Don't worry—though I doubt very strongly that you do—he won't have you arrested. That would cause too much talk. William's reputation is the most important thing in his life. Next to money, that is. And he is definitely not the type to take personal vengeance. He might hire a few dozen men to thrash you within an inch of your life, but he wouldn't come after you himself."

"That's nice to know," Gabe said and decided Corette hadn't told her about the bullet holes in Cabin Number Three.

"Eight o'clock, then," Elaine said. "I look forward to it, Gabe."

Gabe watched her until the bright, green gown disappeared among the trees. Lord God, he thought, if that isn't some kind of woman. Just being with her made his throat go dry. He didn't care to see Robert Porter at all. He had seen the man once and disliked him on sight. Still, Gabe knew he'd have supper with the Devil himself if Elaine agreed to come along, too.

Gabe Conrad had seen more waterfront towns than he cared to remember, and he knew which way to walk. Down past the somber brick warehouses, he found a crooked street without a name. Then, close to the still backwaters of the river, on land that was no use to anyone at all, he found the shacks and campgrounds of the less affluent citizens of Jefferson, Texas.

Snaketown

The first small settlement belonged solely to the blacks. Farther downriver, on slightly higher ground, Gabe came upon the run-down community of the whites. It looked very much like the trash towns that always sprang up near every river port. You could buy cheap whiskey down here and whores who couldn't make it in town. After dark, you could get a knife in the back if your hat and your boots looked new.

Gabe walked into the Steamboat Saloon, a room with weathered lumber walls, planks nailed carelessly together from wrecks that had washed ashore. The ceiling was canvas sooted black from the kerosene lamps down below. Half a dozen men and an oversized girl sat around on boxes and chairs. They all fell silent when Gabe came in. The bartender was a Mexican with a stringy mustache that failed to conceal his rotten teeth.

Gabe ordered a whiskey he didn't intend to drink. In a place like this, a man who wasn't buying wasn't welcome very long.

The bartender served him, looked him over once, and turned away. The girl didn't waste any time. She was at his side at once, her ample breasts pressing firmly against Gabe's arm.

"You come down here for fun, you just run into it, mister," the girl said. "You like to buy me a drink?"

"Get her what she wants," Gabe told the bartender.

The Mexican knew how to do this in his sleep. He poured the girl a shot from a bottle beneath the bar. It was likely colored water, Gabe knew. The idea was to stay cold sober long enough to get a man so drunk he'd take you up to bed. After that, a couple of the girl's good friends would show up to turn you inside out—before or after the action, depending on how the girl felt that afternoon. Gabe didn't intend to stick around for that.

"I'm looking for someone," Gabe said. "Maybe you can help."

The girl grinned. Her teeth weren't as bad as the bartender's, but she had a good start. Her hair was dark as night, and her eyes were coffee-black. Gabe wondered about the hair. It was bright and clean as silk, while the rest of her hadn't seen a bath since spring.

"I can find you 'bout anything you want," the girl said. She leaned in close enough for Gabe to inspect every pore.

"I want a man who knows the swamp country," Gabe told her. "I'll pay top dollar going in and a bonus when he brings me back out. And if I get in there and find he's fooling me around, I won't bring him back at all."

The girl looked startled. She looked quickly over her shoulder, then back at Gabe. "What you want to go in there for, mister? Shit, that's a bad place to be."

"I'm real fond of 'gators." Gabe smiled. "That all right with you? You know anybody or not? Find me someone, and there'll be a little present for you."

The girl liked the idea of that. "How much of a present are we talking 'bout here?"

"How much of a guide you going to find? I don't guess I got your name."

"Louise Ann. You can call me Lou."

"Fine, Lou." Gabe patted her on the butt. "You go find me someone, and we'll talk a little more about you."

The girl nodded and wandered off. Gabe noted she didn't take her drink. He leaned against the bar and watched her in the tarnished mirror. She went to a man in the corner and whispered in his ear. The man listened, looked at Gabe, got up, and walked toward the bar. He was a wiry-looking man near fifty with grizzled cheeks and rheumy eyes. He wore faded overalls with no shirt and no shoes.

"Lou says you're looking for a guide," the man said. "My name's C. R. Cobb, and I reckon I'm your man. If you like, we can have a drink or two, and you can tell me where it is you want to go."

"Have a drink if you like," Gabe said. "Just don't figure it's on me."

"Yeah, well." Cobb's face fell, then he caught himself and grinned. "Guess I'll hold off. Had one a while ago anyway."

"You know the swamp real good, do you, Cobb?"

"Damn right I do. Like the back of my hand, as the man says."

"Good," said Gabe. "I'm sure not looking for some fool who'll get me lost. I need a man who won't drop us off

in a dark hole somewhere, a man who knows the difference between a mud-oak tree and a blue-bark pine."

"You come to the right man," Cobb said. "I can take you anywhere you want. 'Course, I know you expect to pay good— I mean, to get a man who really knows his trade."

"I will if I find him," Gabe said. "I know damn sure it isn't you. I never even heard of a blue-bark pine or a mud-oak either, Mr. Cobb. I got an idea the only swamp you've seen is in your head."

Cobb's face flushed with anger. Then, he decided getting mad wasn't too good an idea, considering Gabe's size.

"Don't know why you can't take a joke," Cobb muttered. "Didn't mean anything by it, you understand."

"I sure do," Gabe said.

Cobb stalked hurriedly past Gabe and disappeared out the front door. Gabe tossed a few coins on the bar and walked out himself. Lou caught up with him in the street.

"Listen, I'm sorry 'bout Cobb," she said. "Hell, he told me he knew the swamp. I should've knowed better. That bastard's about as big a liar as there is."

Gabe pressed two dollars in the girl's hand. "You made a mistake is all, Lou. You care to make an honest five to go with the two, you rustle me up a real guide. My name's Conrad, and I'm staying at the Excelsior Hotel."

The girl blinked. "I been in there once."

"Fine. Then you know where it is."

Gabe walked back the way he'd come. The afternoon shadows were stretching into evening, and he guessed it was time to get ready for Mr. Robert Porter and Elaine. He wondered what she'd wear. Not the green dress; he'd already seen that, and Elaine wasn't a lady who'd likely wear the same dress twice. Not on the very same day.

As he left the shacks of trash town behind and started back up the hill, a figure darted into a doorway to his right. Gabe stopped and looked. He had only glimpsed the man for a second, but he was certain that he'd recognized the loud plaid suit. He wondered if Holzer had followed him from town, or if he had some business here himself?

CHAPTER NINE

Night was settling in by the time Gabe reached the Excelsior Hotel. After spotting Holzer in the backwater settlement, he was glad to leave the dark pathways by the river and return to the center of town. The main streets of Jefferson were brightly lit. Pine-knot gas burned in glass globes atop high, ornate lampposts, furnishing a cheery light for the well-dressed men and women who walked along the avenues. Laughter came from the carriages that rattled by; an attractive young woman shared a secret smile with Gabe before her surrey disappeared.

Gabe wondered if this lady knew a whole different world existed less than ten minutes away. Likely not, he decided. And if she did, she wouldn't let it disturb her pretty thoughts.

Gabe's belly felt hollow as a drum. He was tempted to stop at one of the sidewalk stalls selling lemonade and sizzling strips of beef wrapped in bread, but decided to hold off until supper. Earlier, he'd taken a look at the Excelsior's lavish menu, and the wondrous items there seemed well worth the wait.

Another hot bath seemed a good idea, but he settled for washing up from the basin in his room. After putting on his

brand new shirt, he dusted off his trousers and wiped his boots, looped the holster around his shoulder, and put on his denim jacket. It might not be what Elaine Porter and her father considered evening wear, but Gabe figured it would have to do.

He was slicking back his hair with his hand when a heavy fist drummed on his door. Gabe stepped quickly to one side.

"What do you want?" he said.

"It's Jake Harper," said a voice from outside. "I need to see you, Conrad."

Gabe cursed under his breath and opened up. Harper stepped in, looked Gabe over, and gave him a sullen look.

"Stepping out on the town, are you? Well, ain't that nice?"

Gabe ignored the man. He peered in the mirror and brushed a spot of dust off his sleeve.

"Sheriff, you know damn well what I'm doing," he said. "I'm having supper downstairs with Elaine Porter and her father. I expect you know what we'll have to eat and the waiter's first name. What do want to see me about?"

Harper leaned against the dresser and folded his arms.

"That wasn't a good idea. Hanging out down by the river. A man can get himself in trouble down there."

Gabe grinned. "I bet you been talking to the lovely Lou. The girl's a real charmer, I got to say that."

"I talk to lots of folks. I do my job, and I do it right. I know what's going on in Jefferson, Texas."

"I don't doubt it for a minute."

Harper made a noise in his throat. "There's men here who could guide you into the swamp. You keep askin' you'll find one or two. But they won't take you in. They'll find they've got other things to do."

"You'll make sure of that."

Harper shrugged. "Now I can't help it if a man doesn't want to do a job. That isn't any business of mine."

Gabe turned and faced Harper. "Mister, you ever talk straight? Or have you been beating around the bush so long you flat forgot how?"

Harper went rigid and the color rose to his face. For an instant, Gabe figured they'd go at it right there, tearing up

the Excelsior's fancy room. Then, Harper let out a breath and shook his head.

"If I had any reason to run you out of town then I would," he told Gabe. "I don't, so I'll spell it out plain. I don't blame you for wanting to get even. I guess I'd feel the same. That's a hell of a thing, an old man gettin' torn in half like that. I know this Caddo Jack and how he thinks. Even if Mr. Porter's brother hadn't made a dumb move, Jack might've shot him anyway. Or the whole lot of you, for that matter. He kills 'cause he likes it. It's what he does for fun. Stealing's just something he does because there's something there to take."

Harper paused and looked past Gabe. Bugs circled crazily about a streetlamp outside.

"Caddo Jack hides out in the Thicket," Harper went on. "You got any idea what kind of place that is? The swamp's so full of woods and brush, you can't go half a mile in a day. I can't even say how many hundred thousand acres we're talking about here. There's places in there *no*body's ever been, not even the Indians. What the hell gives you the gall, mister, to think you could find Caddo Jack? Shit—you'd just as well go lookin' for a particular rattlesnake. There's about two jillion of 'em there, and all you're hunting for is one."

"You've made your point," Gabe said. "I sure can't say you're wrong."

"But you figure on trying it anyway, right?" Harper stood and looked Gabe squarely in the eye. "You do, and you'll do it on your own. Won't anybody in this town give you any help. What's Mr. Porter want to see you about, anyway? Whatever it is, I'd mind my manners if I was you. Isn't anything in Jefferson worth owning, Mr. Porter doesn't have a slice or two of."

Gabe smiled. "Wondered when you'd get around to it."

"Get around to what?"

"What you came busting in here for. Anybody pees in Jefferson, you've got to know how much. I'm having supper with the town's big cheese, and you don't know why, and that sticks in your craw."

A storm brewed in Jake Harper's eyes. For the second time in five minutes, Gabe thought the man was about to cut loose.

Gabe half hoped he would. He was getting tired of waiting for the other shoe to drop.

"Hell with you, mister," Harper said finally. "I don't give a damn who you eat supper with, 'long as it's not me."

Color still spotting his cheeks, Harper brushed past Gabe and stomped out.

Gabe dropped a couple of dollars in his pocket and found his key, then started downstairs. It wasn't any big surprise that the sheriff had a real short fuse. Gabe had known that the first time he laid eyes on the man. What he hadn't seen clearly till now, was just how strongly Harper felt about Elaine. He was more than just interested in Porter's daughter, he was plain crazy about her. He didn't care if Gabe and Porter had breakfast in bed. What made him angry enough to chew nails was that Elaine was going to be there at supper as well.

Can't say I blame him, Gabe thought. If I had to look at that woman every day and think about her half the night, I'd more than likely lose my mind, too.

Supper was everything Gabe expected, and then some. The evening started off with wild duck with plum sauce, crawfish cooked in butter and garlic and served in a good wine sauce, roast pork with mint jelly, fried chicken, mashed potatoes, candied yams, fresh green beans, corn on the cob, fried green tomatoes, and two or three different kinds of wine. Gabe ignored the wine, but devoured everything else that came along. After the plates were cleared away, the waiter brought coffee, vanilla ice cream, chocolate cake, and hot cherry pie with a slab of melted cheddar on top.

It was, Gabe decided, one of the finest meals he'd ever had. Further, tasting each new delight gave him something to do besides stare at Elaine. Elaine hadn't made it real easy for any normal male to pay attention to his food. For the evening, she had swept her dark hair up in a coil atop her head and let a curl or two sweep down on either cheek. She wore a white silk gown that made Gabe want to cry. The white was a perfect contrast to her honey-colored flesh, and the neckline of the dress came dangerously close to allowing her swelling treasures to spring free.

Gabe did the best he could to keep from looking, but it was no easy task. Elaine knew exactly what he was doing and didn't seem to mind. Now and then she looked right at him, smiling with her deep, green eyes. Gabe would have bet a hundred dollars that Harper was brooding somewhere out in the dark, trying to decide how he might drop this intruder down a well and still stay within the law.

Robert Porter said little at all until the plates were all gone and the waiter had filled their cups with fresh coffee. He lit a long cheroot, blew out a plume of blue smoke, and looked directly at Gabe.

"Wasn't my idea, us having supper together," he said shortly. "Daughter talked me into it. Guess she could talk me into sawing off my leg."

"Now, Father." She blushed politely and smiled at Gabe. "What an awful thing to say."

"Well, I sure thank you for the meal," Gabe said. "It was real fine, Mr. Porter."

Porter waved Gabe's thanks away. "Let me say one thing right off," he said. "I strongly disapprove of your action with Mr. William Clay. Probably had it coming to him. But that doesn't make it right. Now, that's done." Porter leaned across the table at Gabe. "What can you tell me about my brother? I'd be obliged if you'd tell me anything he might have said."

"We didn't talk all that much," Gabe told him. "He said it was his first trip to Jefferson. That he—uh, didn't expect to be making the trip. He said he—what? He said, about the time you think you know where you stand, you find out that isn't the way things are. Something like that."

Porter frowned into his coffee, then pointed his cheroot at Gabe. "I never sent that letter," he said flatly. "That invitation didn't come from me, I'll tell you that."

"Who do you think did?" Gabe asked. "Can you think of anyone who'd have a reason for using your name? For wanting to get your brother up here?"

"Hmmmph!" Porter shook his head. "Most likely, the old fool wrote it himself. Sounds like something he'd do. Man drank to excess, always did. Doubt if he changed his habits, likely got worse. Wrote the damn letter to himself and didn't

have the sense to remember what he did."

It seemed like an unlikely answer to Gabe, but he let the point pass. "Mind if I ask, Mr. Porter? When did you see your brother last?"

"Been close to thirty years," Porter said. "Didn't figure the man was still alive." Porter paused, then looked narrowly at Gabe. "I know what you're thinking, Mr. Conrad. I can read a man like a book. If you were trying to sell me timber, I could tell you to the penny what you'd take. You're thinking if I haven't seen Josh in all that time, how do I know what he's like, or what he'd do. I'll tell you, mister—people don't change, that's how. I knew him then, and I know him now. I know what he was, and by God I know he died the same worthless son of a bitch he was thirty years ago!"

Gabe started to speak, but Porter cut him off.

"Just listen, young man. I'll let you know when I'm through. I'm going to tell you something now. Then I'm going to tell you why I did. Thirty years ago, Josh and I were trading goods in Tennessee. He was 'bout forty, and I was twenty something. Josh was my brother, but he treated me no better than a nigger slave. When Josh spit, I jumped. I would've shot him in the back if I'd ever got the nerve, but he had me cowed good. You get the tar beat out of you enough, you learn to keep your mouth shut.

"One summer night south of Nashville, Josh got drunk and raped a Cherokee girl. Hurt her real bad and left her for dead. The girl's father came looking for Josh, and Josh shot him in the head. Didn't give the man a chance, just killed him on the spot. I got Josh on a horse and led him off into the woods before the law could catch up. I saw him lyin' there half drunk and throwing up on himself, and it hit me that I couldn't take any more of that. Couldn't, and didn't have to. I took my share of our goods and money and left. That's the last time I saw him until today. What I should've done is turn him over to the law. Let 'em hang the bastard."

Porter noisily sipped his coffee. "I have regretted that decision ever since."

Gabe couldn't think what to say. He looked at Elaine. Elaine was biting her lip, staring down at her hands.

"I can see how you'd feel that way," Gabe said finally. "Must have been a real hurtful thing for you, thinking about that for all these years, then seeing your brother turn up here under unpleasant circumstances."

Porter looked curiously at Gabe, then showed him a sober smile. "Then you'd be wrong as you can be, Mr. Conrad. I haven't given Josh Porter more than a passing thought since I left him drunk under a tree. Now he's dead, and I am forced to think about him again."

Porter made a face, like he'd tasted something bad. "I do not like things unfinished. Ask anyone you like. They'll tell you Robert Porter is a man who never leaves a task half done. That is my nature, sir. I am not content until all the i's are dotted and all the t's are crossed. And that is precisely where you come in."

Gabe looked puzzled. "Mr. Porter, I guess you lost me somewhere. I don't get what you're saying."

Porter crushed his cigar in a saucer. "Elaine tells me you intend to go after this Caddo Jack. I am willing to add some incentive to your search. If you bring him in dead, I will pay you what you ask. You name the price. I was thinking in the neighborhood of five thousand dollars. If that is not suitable . . ." Porter shrugged, as if such a sum would certainly be suitable to anyone.

Gabe stared. He fought to try and hold back his anger. Damn the man! He thought everything came with a price. Whatever the hell it was, you could buy it by the bale.

"I don't want your money, Mr. Porter," Gabe said, bringing all the calm he could muster into his voice. "I don't know what kind of man your brother used to be or what he did. I know he took a lot of lead for me, and that's all I need to know."

Porter leaned back and grinned, showing Gabe a fine set of store-bought teeth. "Then you and I are in agreement, Mr. Conrad. Killing Caddo Jack is a point of honor with you. Just as it's a point of honor with me."

"Pardon me if I don't believe that," Gabe said evenly. "Near as I can tell, you don't give a damn that your brother's dead. There isn't any honor in that."

"Oh, don't get me wrong," Porter said. "You are quite correct. I *don't* give a damn that he's dead. I am not concerned with his honor, sir. He didn't have any to lose, as far as I can see. It is *my* honor we're talking about here. Some half-breed has murdered a member of my family, a man with the same name as mine. And that is a reflection on me, something I cannot abide. I will not rest until I know that killer is dead."

Gabe glanced at Elaine. He couldn't tell what she was thinking. Her expression gave nothing away.

"I want to thank you again for the supper, Mr. Porter," Gabe said. "I appreciate the invitation."

Porter laughed and stood. "No, you don't. You're mad enough to kick me in the butt. If Elaine wasn't here I expect you would."

"Long as we're being honest, the thought had crossed my mind," Gabe said.

"Good, that's the sport," Porter said. "A man who doesn't say what he thinks isn't worth a plugged nickel in my book."

Porter dropped a handful of money on the table. Gabe wasn't sure he bothered to count.

Gabe followed Porter and his daughter outside. A carriage waited by the curb, a black driver at the reins. Porter saw a friend he knew and stopped to say hello.

Elaine came quickly up to Gabe. "I'm sorry," she said, resting one hand on Gabe's arm. "I encouraged him, I'm afraid. I thought—I didn't mean to offend you. Honestly I didn't."

"Don't think anything of it," Gabe said.

"But I do, though. Sometimes Father can be a little—abrupt? Is that the right word?"

"That'll do for now," Gabe grinned. "And don't worry any about me. Your father's got a way of looking at things and—*son of a bitch!*"

Gabe grabbed Elaine by the shoulder and tossed her roughly to the ground. In the same instant, his hand snaked under his arm and came up with the Colt. The three riders came around the corner fast. Gabe recognized Holzer in the lead. Brightness flared from Holzer's gun, and Gabe felt lead tug at his sleeve. He snapped off a shot, but had to hold off a second for fear of hitting Porter. The other two riders opened fire, and glass

shattered in the Excelsior's door. Gabe ran past the carriage into the street. Holzer was lost in the dark, but Gabe fired twice at the next rider. He slumped in the saddle and fell heavily into the dirt. A surprise shot came from across the street, and the second man cried out and dropped.

Gabe stopped in his tracks and saw Jake Harper walk out of the shadows, slipping his gun back into its holster.

Harper glanced up the street and walked over to Gabe.

"Seems like you could eat supper without disturbing the peace," Harper said. "You get the chocolate cake or the pie?"

"Both," Gabe said. "And vanilla ice cream."

Harper looked solemnly at Gabe. "You want to tell me what the hell's going on here or not? Everything was real friendly in Jefferson 'fore you got in town."

"And I don't recall getting shot at before I ate in your fine hotel," Gabe said. "You might ought to think on that."

CHAPTER TEN

Elaine had a slight bruise on her arm and a tear in her gown. Otherwise, she was none the worse for wear. Employees of the Excelsior Hotel immediately rushed her into the lobby and brought her hot tea. Gabe found her there, pale, and somewhat shaken. A strand of dark hair, loosened by her fall, hung carelessly over her bare shoulder. Gabe was taken aback by the effect. Elaine in slight disarray was even more alluring than Elaine perfectly dressed for an evening out. He wondered what this woman would have to do to look bad. You could drop her in a pigpen, and she'd come out looking grand.

"You all right?" Gabe said. "You're not hurt or anything, are you?"

"I'm fine," Elaine said. "I'm still a little scared, is all."

"Well, you've got a right to be, after something like that. I'm sorry I had to push you down so hard. I couldn't think of anything else to do."

Elaine laid a hand on Gabe's arm and held him with her enormous green eyes. "Gabe, please don't apologize for saving my life, all right? I think I—Lord, those terrible men! Why were they shooting at us? I simply don't understand!"

"I don't think it was *us*," Gabe said. "More likely it was me. One of the riders was a man I had a run-in with on the boat."

"I don't think you're suited to riverboat travel, Gabe Conrad." Elaine showed him a weary smile. "You appear to have trouble finding good traveling companions."

"I wish I'd have walked, if that's what you mean. Listen, you just sit here and rest. You need anything, I'll be right outside."

"It's nice to know that, Gabe." Elaine gave him a look that he felt clear down to his toes. He didn't want to leave; he wanted to stay right where he was.

When Gabe walked outside again, he found the street full of people. It was nearly eleven at night, but it looked as if everyone in Jefferson had found their way to the center of town. In the middle of the crowd was Robert Porter. He was perched atop a box, shouting out orders to anyone who'd stand still and listen. From what Gabe could hear, Porter had called every man to arms. If a man didn't own a weapon or a horse, Porter would make sure he got these items for the night. Every able-bodied man, by God, would rally to the call, or Porter would know the reason why.

Gabe found Sheriff Jake Harper across the street, leaning on a hitching post and rolling himself a smoke. He gave Gabe a sour look and scratched a lucifer on his boot.

"Elaine all right?" Harper asked. "She didn't get hurt, I don't guess."

"Good as new," Gabe said.

"Real nice of you to take the time to comfort the lady. Don't know how we managed 'fore you came along."

"Well, there doesn't seem to be a whole lot to do," Gabe said. "Mr. Porter's recruiting himself an army. Looks like everything's under control."

Harper squinted narrowly at Gabe and muttered something under his breath. "I've got seven deputies out trying to run that fella down. They'll get him, most likely, if Mr. Porter don't send a hundred greenhorns out to shoot each other in the dark. Isn't much I can do about that. Mr. Porter's a real proud

man, and he doesn't take kindly to being shot at. Especially in his own town. I got a look at the one that got away. He came in on the boat with you. You want to tell me anything about that?"

"His name's Holzer. He's some kind of scam artist, near as I can tell."

"And you had trouble with him on the *Cypress Moon*?"

"We didn't get along real well."

"You get him riled enough to pull a stunt like this?"

Gabe hesitated. He wondered if he ought to tell Harper he had seen Holzer sneaking around in trash town earlier in the evening. He decided it wouldn't do much good. It wouldn't help Harper catch him any faster, and that was all that really counted now.

"I don't know," Gabe said finally. "I think it'd make Holzer happy if he could back-shoot me somewhere and get away with it. I'm a little surprised to see him trying out in the open. Who were the other two? Anybody you know?"

"Both of 'em. Couple of local toughs who'd do most anything for a couple of dollars and a drink."

"Hope they got paid first," Gabe said. "Anything I can do to help?"

Harper gave Gabe a rueful look. "You could tell me if you angered anyone else on the *Cypress Moon* I haven't heard about yet. That'd be a help. Otherwise, I'd like you to stay the hell out of my way."

Gabe smiled. "I think I can handle that." He started to walk away, then stopped. "I appreciate you bringing one of those boys down. Real good shot. Nice you happened to be close by."

Harper swelled up like a toad, and Gabe knew he'd guessed right. The sheriff had been standing across the street all the time, watching Elaine have supper and nursing his anger through every course.

"You keep pushing me, and you'll find you got your hands full, mister," Harper said. "I'd keep that in mind if I was you."

"I'll sure do that, Sheriff," Gabe said, then walked back across the street to the hotel.

• • •

"It was kind of you to see us home," Elaine said as they rode home in the carriage. "It wasn't really necessary, Gabe. I'm certain we're in no danger now."

"My privilege," Gabe said. "I feel like it's kind of my fault you folks were troubled this evening."

"Damn right it was," Porter grumbled.

"Father!" Elaine brought a hand up to the vee of her dress and looked appalled. "I do not see how you can blame Mr. Conrad. He certainly did not *invite* those men to attack him. He is just as upset over the affair as you are."

"Hmmph!" said Porter.

Gabe leaned back in his seat and watched the streets and darkened houses go by. Robert Porter and Elaine sat in shadow directly across from him. He could see Elaine's face, the flesh of her shoulders and the ghostly white color of her gown. Occasionally, the oaks overhead thinned enough to let him see her eyes. He was certain she was looking right at him, that she could see him in the night.

Gabe wondered if she knew what he was thinking. If she did, all that bare skin would turn red as a beet. Or maybe it wouldn't, he decided. A woman bold enough to look right at a man the way she did might very well be bold enough to have some fanciful thoughts of her own.

Gabe savored this idea until the carriage pulled into a long gravel drive and came to a halt. The Porter home was bigger than the Excelsior Hotel, a large, columned, white structure set amid live oaks and magnolias as old as the country itself.

"Marshall will run you back," Porter said. "You didn't have to come, but I'm obliged."

"Thank you," Gabe said, "but I'd just as soon walk, you don't mind. Air'll do me good."

"Suit yourself," Porter said gruffly. "I'm getting a whiskey and going to bed. Sorriest evening I ever had. And that duck was too damn sweet, you ask me. Fool chef drowns everything in sauce."

Porter climbed the steps of his house. A black man in uniform opened the door at once, and Porter disappeared inside.

The carriage pulled off toward the back of the house, and Gabe was left alone with Elaine. The night had brought a reasonably cool breeze through the town, and Gabe could smell honeysuckle nearby.

"I'd like you to come in and see the house, but it's getting kind of late," Elaine said. "Will you promise to come by another time?"

"I'll sure take you up on that," Gabe said. "You get some rest, now. I expect you're—"

"Gabe?"

Elaine came closer and rested both hands on his shoulders. Gabe inhaled the tantalizing scent of her hair.

"Gabe," Elaine said softly, "are you really going after the man who killed my uncle? You haven't changed your mind?"

"Now I don't know why I'd do that, Elaine. It's something I feel I have to do."

"I thought—" Elaine wet her lips. "Well, after tonight and everything. Those men shooting at you and all . . ."

Gabe shook his head. "That business didn't have anything to do with your uncle. If you're thinking Holzer might try for me again, you can put that thought out of your head. He isn't going to bother me again. If he doesn't get caught, he'll hightail it out of here, as far from Jefferson as he can get."

Elaine was silent a moment, then she looked up at Gabe and slid her hands around his neck. Her eyes were closed, and her face was turned up to his. When Gabe's lips touched hers, he felt a tremor surge through his body. She parted her lips to welcome him in. Gabe tasted every sweet hollow of delight. His every touch seemed to stoke the fires within her. With a sharp little cry, she went limp against him. Gabe let his mouth caress her lips and her cheeks, then trail through the silk of her hair to the column of her throat.

"Oh, Gabe!" Elaine cried. Her nails dug into his back, then she slipped her hands tightly around his head and guided his lips to her breasts.

The moment his mouth touched the soft and yielding flesh, Elaine gasped, gripped his shoulders, and gently pushed him back.

"Oh God, we—we can't, Gabe. Not right—right here on Father's lawn!"

"I'll bet I can find us someplace," Gabe said. "It's dark as pitch out here and won't anybody—"

"Gabe . . ." Elaine smiled and touched a finger to his lips. "We will. I promise you that. But not now. Oh, Gabe, I promise you we will!"

Elaine stretched up on her toes and kissed him lightly on the mouth. Gabe reached for her again, and she playfully slipped through his grasp. He watched her run up the steps and inside. He could still taste her mouth, still feel her body pressed against him. He ached all over, but the hurt seemed centered in one particular spot. He wondered if he could walk back to the hotel. It wasn't more than six or eight blocks. Still . . .

By God, he thought irritably, all I did was kiss the woman, and she's left me weak as a sick dog. He looked up at the house once more; he imagined Elaine getting undressed for bed, and wondered what she was wearing—or if she was wearing anything at all. Then he turned and quickly walked away. With my luck, he decided, Holzer will pop up from behind a tree and knock me over with a switch. All he'd have to do is just—

Gabe went rigid as a terrible cry broke the stillness of the night. The scream turned him cold and raised the hackles on his neck.

"Elaine!" he shouted and started running back toward the house.

A kerosene lamp came to life downstairs, then another in a second story window. The front door was locked. Gabe stepped back, aimed a boot, and kicked it in. A frightened servant stood in the hall, gazing at the long stairway to the right. Gabe bounded up the flight of stairs, hitting every fourth step. The hallway turned to the left and to the right.

"Elaine, where the hell are you?" Gabe yelled.

A low, piercing cry came from the left; Gabe whipped the Colt from under his coat and ran in that direction. Elaine stumbled out of a room and fell into his arms. Gabe scarcely recognized the girl. Terror had twisted her features into someone he didn't know.

Gabe lifted Elaine in his arms, set her in a hallway chair, and went cautiously into the room, the Colt held steadily in his hand. At once, he smelled the awful odor of death. Grabbing a lamp from a table, he crossed the room and saw her on the bed.

Gabe winced and bile rose up in his throat. Corette Clay lay naked across the bed. Someone had used a sharp knife to slit her open from her crotch right up to her throat. Everything inside was spilling out. Her body was a pale, unnatural shade of blue, and Gabe saw nearly all the blood in her body had soaked into the sheets.

A voice behind Gabe made him turn. Robert Porter stood in the doorway in his nightshirt, blinking against the light.

"Don't come in here," Gabe said harshly. He grabbed the old man and turned him around. "Take care of Elaine. See that she's all right. Clay, Corette's husband. Was he staying in this room, too?"

"D-down the hall," Porter mumbled. "What—what's happening here!"

Gabe didn't answer. He ran down the hallway, flinging open doors. The third one belonged to William Clay. Gabe stepped inside, closed his eyes a moment, and let out a long breath. Rough-hewn beams formed heavy rafters in the high-ceilinged room. William Clay hung naked by his heels, attached to a beam by a short length of rope. He swung gently from side to side, his fingers nearly touching the floor. He was slit open exactly like his wife, drained and empty as a side of heavy beef. Gabe thought the man didn't look mad at anyone anymore.

CHAPTER ELEVEN

At two o'clock the following afternoon, a funeral procession rolled solemnly through town to the Jefferson cemetery. An announcement posted at the funeral parlor made it clear that the services would be private, for "friends and family members only." This excluded everyone except Robert Porter and his daughter, Elaine, which was exactly as Porter himself had intended.

Nevertheless, every man, woman, and child within thirty miles of Jefferson showed up for the ceremonies. They came in fine carriages, in farm wagons, on horseback, and on foot. Many brought picnic suppers and camping gear. After all, it wasn't every day you could witness the burial of not one, but three mutilated murder victims.

A large number of those attending had gathered in the town's saloons to discuss the grisly deaths of Joshua Porter and William and Corette Clay. And by the hour of the funeral itself, quite a few were well fortified with drink, and felt it would be a fine gesture of respect to fire off their weapons in the air.

To add to the problem of drunks, lost children, and a massive traffic jam, a thunderstorm swept over the town at a quarter till three, turning the roads—which had scarcely dried out from the

rain two days before—into churning rivers of mud. It was nearly six-thirty before Sheriff Jake Harper and his beleaguered deputies brought the town back to some semblance of order.

Gabe Conrad had spent most of the long night at the Porter home, helping out in any way he could. Immediately after discovery of the slaughtered victims, servants were dispatched to bring a doctor and Sheriff Harper to the scene. Elaine had passed out in the hall; Gabe felt this was a blessing, since he had his hands full with her father. Robert Porter completely lost control of his senses. It was all Gabe could do to hold him down until help arrived. The doctor took one look at the man and filled him with enough opiates to fell a horse.

When Elaine came around, she insisted on taking care of her father. The doctor felt he ought to drug her, too, but Elaine would have none of that. Gabe thought she was unusually calm and likely in a state of shock.

At six in the morning, Gabe walked back to the Excelsior Hotel and fell in bed. He slept until noon, ate a big breakfast, and went out looking for Jake Harper. Harper, however, was still trying to put his town back together and had little time to talk.

Gabe didn't run the sheriff down until seven that evening. Harper was eating supper at a café near his office and looked as if he'd tangled with a bear and come out with second prize. Gabe didn't care much for the man, but he knew what Harper had been through, and that he hadn't been to bed for some time.

"I figure we ought to talk," Gabe said, "but we sure don't have to do it now."

"Sit down," Harper said wearily. "I plan on shootin' myself at eight, so now's as good a time as it's going to get."

Gabe ordered coffee and watched Harper wolf down a steak. "Hasn't been a real fine day for you, I know that," he said. "Looks as if things are settling down some, though."

Harper speared a piece of beef and looked at Gabe. "I got a jail full of rowdies, half a dozen people in the hospital, including two of my own men. I got a woman from Tyler having twins, and about twenty vehicles broke down on the roads. On

the other hand, everybody in town that's got a store of any sort is carting money to the bank. It's sorta like Christmas and the Fourth of July, all happening at once. Shit, my pa wanted me to go into cotton like him. I wish to hell I'd listened to the man."

Gabe glanced past Harper to the street outside. The clouds had scudded away and left the town in eerie light.

"I expect you've been thinking about the same thing as me," he said. "I thought we might talk about that. I don't guess there's any doubt it was Caddo Jack who cut up the Clays. You see it that way, too?"

Harper nodded. "I don't figure we've got more'n one maniac on the loose. I hope to God we don't."

The sheriff paused and looked thoughtfully at Gabe. "I know what you're getting at, mister. A killing on the river's one thing, but two more is somethin' else. I'm not real big on coincidences, and this whole business smells rotten as bad meat. Caddo Jack kills Mr. Porter's brother, then he breaks in and kills the Clays—"

"He could just as easily have waited till Porter and Elaine got home from supper and killed them," Gabe finished. "But he didn't. He murdered the Clays instead. Now why'd he do that? The way things are shaping up, I'm thinking it wasn't chance that Caddo Jack shot Joshua Porter on the *Cypress Moon*. Josh jumped up and took the shot, I know that, and I thought he was taking it for me."

"I think you're right. I think that half-breed would've shot the old man anyway."

"Unless I'm off the track, I'm saying he killed Josh Porter for the same reason he picked out the Clays. To scare the hell out of Robert Porter. The thing is, I don't know why. Someone wrote that letter to get Josh up here. Caddo Jack did the killing, but I doubt he's got anything to do with the letter. Someone else did that and used Caddo Jack to do the dirty work." Gabe let out a breath. "That son of a bitch Holzer's in this somewhere. I'd bet my roll on that."

Harper frowned and shook his head. "Wait a minute," he said, "you don't know anything of the kind. Holzer was after *you*. I was there, remember? That doesn't tie him into the rest of this mess."

"Uh-huh. And all this happens about the same time that Caddo Jack's out hacking folks up at Porter's house. And Porter and Elaine are conveniently out of the way, eating supper with me. No, Holzer had it in for me, all right, and I'm sure he jumped at the chance to gun me down. But someone told him to do it, Sheriff."

Harper made a face. "Yeah, and who would that be?"

"I don't have the slightest idea. But I do recall something that hadn't crossed my mind before. Just before Caddo Jack came aboard the *Cypress Moon*, I ran into Holzer on deck. He was sitting out a hand in that poker game, leaning over the railing, and looking at the river. I didn't think anything of it at the time. Now I'm thinking he was waiting for someone."

"Caddo Jack, I suppose."

"Right. Caddo Jack. Hell, Harper, Josh Porter, the man I knew as Lucas Harrow, made it clear to me that Holzer was dogging him all the way up to Jefferson. Holzer was on the train with him coming up from Baton Rouge to Shreveport. He might've been following him before that."

Jake Harper scratched his two-day-old beard. "Sounds all tied up real neat and tidy the way you put it, but I'm not buying Holzer in this. You're linking a lot of stuff together that's pure guesswork and nothing more than that."

"You're the one who doesn't like coincidences," Gabe reminded him. "You tell me anything else that makes sense. I'll be glad to change my mind."

"I don't have any answers, and you know it," Harper said shortly. "That don't mean yours are right. Who'd want to *do* a thing like this? What's the point of killing three people to scare Mr. Porter? What for?"

Harper ran his hands through his hair and gave Gabe a sour look. "Shit, listen to me. I'm so damn tired my head's quit working right. I'm sitting here listening to you 'cause I haven't got the sense to go to bed."

Gabe refused to give in. "You were with me, friend, right up to the part about Holzer. If you can buy someone behind Caddo Jack, and that's a lot to swallow, you ought to be able to make room for Holzer."

"Get out of here, Conrad, and leave me alone," Harper said crossly. "Likely doesn't matter if I believe you or not. After that three-ring circus at the cemetery, I doubt if I got a job anymore. Mr. Porter doesn't care much for things that don't go his way."

The last of the day had disappeared by the time Gabe walked back from the café to his hotel. The pine-knot lamps were burning bright, and the streets were a sea of mud. The board sidewalks were full of people, and the saloons were overflowing with men who had gathered for the day's big event. Gabe wondered how many still remembered what they'd come to town to see.

Shedding his clothes on the floor, Gabe dropped wearily into bed. He wondered how Elaine was doing. He was sure she hadn't slept the night before. Hopefully, the shock of what she'd seen had worn off by now, and she had managed to get some rest.

For the first time since he'd heard Elaine screaming through the night, he remembered what had happened between them moments before. He had watched her all through supper, thinking how it would be to touch her, to hold her in his arms. Then, outside the Porter home, it was Elaine who had come to him, Elaine who had laid her hands on his shoulders, inviting him to kiss her, and promising a great deal more than that.

Gabe dropped off thinking how the evening might have gone, instead of how it did. In the dream that carried him restlessly into sleep, Elaine held his hand and led him into the darkened house. In her room, he stood and watched as she slipped out of her gown in the moonlight and walked into his arms. He felt her skin burning against him and realized he was somehow naked already and didn't have to shed his clothes. Elaine took him to her bed. He caressed her dark hair, kissed her, and suddenly felt dead lips against his own. He jerked back in horror and saw it was Corette in his arms, cold eyes staring into his. He screamed as William Clay dropped heavily from the ceiling, grabbed him, and started gnawing on his head.

Gabe sat up with a start, staring into the night. His heart beat wildly against his chest. In a moment, he realized someone was

knocking, tapping lightly and whispering his name.

Pulling himself up, he slipped into his trousers and picked up the Colt on the way.

"Who is it?" he said. "What the hell do you want?"

"Gabe? It's me. Let me in, please."

"Elaine?" Gabe blinked at the door, wondering if he might still be asleep. He turned the key in the lock, peered out, and saw her standing in the dark.

"Gabe, would you please open this door? I don't want everyone in town to see me standing out here."

"Right. Come on in." Gabe stood back and rubbed the sleep from his eyes. In the light from the street, he saw she was dressed in an old blue work shirt and jeans that were much too tight. Her hair was tucked under an oversized straw hat.

Gabe had to grin. "If you think anyone's going to take you for a mule skinner, lady, you've got another guess coming."

"I did the best I could," Elaine snapped. "I'm not used to this, you know. Oh, Gabe, just hold me a minute, will you? I'm so scared I don't know what to do!"

Gabe took her in his arms. Her face turned up to his, and he kissed her hard. He could feel the warmth of her tears against his cheek. Her hands tightened against his back and drew him close. Gabe slid his hand from her waist to the swell of her hips.

Elaine caught her breath and pulled away, then rested her head against his chest.

"Oh Lord, Gabe, I'm so glad you're here. I—please, give me a minute, all right? I want you something awful, but I've got to just try and get myself together some first."

"I can understand that," Gabe said. "You've been through a lot. How's your father? He doing all right?"

Elaine sank down on the bed and looked at her hands. "I don't even know him anymore, Gabe. He's—he's gone off somewhere. There's nothing but fear in his eyes. He just sits there in his chair like he's already dead or something. I'm not sure he knows who I am anymore."

"He'll come around. The shock of last night—"

"No." Elaine shook her head. "I'm not sure he'll ever be the same. Something's gotten to him. I don't know what, but it's

not just about what happened to William and Corette and Uncle Josh . . ."

Elaine glanced up helplessly at Gabe. "I'm terribly frightened, Gabe. I'm afraid of something, and I don't know what it is."

Elaine reached out and took his hand and guided Gabe down beside her. "Listen to me, Gabe. Please. Just listen to me a while and let me say what it is I have to say. You're not going to like it very much, but listen to me anyway."

"All right." Gabe tried to read the expression in her eyes. "I'm listening, Elaine."

"I can take you into the swamp. I used to go fishing in there when I was a child. Old Jim, the colored man who worked for us then, used to take me in there all the time. Father would take us with him when he had some business to do south of here, and I know the—"

"Now wait a minute, Elaine . . ."

"No, now you said you'd hear me out. Old Jim told me a lot of things. About the way people live in there, and what they do. There are settlements in there, Gabe, whole towns tucked away in the swamp. People who live out most of their lives in the Thicket."

"Right," Gabe said, "and they live in there because they don't want to have anything to do with strangers. That means you and me."

Elaine held Gabe with her eyes. "I wouldn't exactly be a stranger, Gabe. They'll let me in. My mother's out there."

Gabe stared. "What are you talking about? You don't know where your mother is."

"Yes, I do, though. I told you she wasn't from Father's class of folks. That's where she came from, one of the settlements in the Thicket. And that's where she went when she ran away."

Gabe pressed her hand between his. "Do you know that, or is that where you think she is? Your mother might not have gone back. She could be most anywhere."

"I know, Gabe. I do."

"How do you know?"

Elaine looked away. "I just do, Gabe. Believe me, I do. And when I find her—when you help me find her—you can get all

the guides you want to go after Caddo Jack. Mother's friends will help you all they can."

"You're getting way ahead of yourself," Gabe said. "Supposing I did take you with me, which I won't. Supposing your mother just happens to be in the Thicket, which you're only hoping that she is. If we could even find her, Elaine, which I've got a lot of doubts about . . ." Gabe let his words trail off. "You're building a whole lot out of not much, Elaine. I think you've got to see that."

Elaine pulled her hand away. "I'm going, Gabe. Whether you take me or not. I should've gone before. I just kept thinking about it and not doing anything. I've got a whole life behind me full of questions. Father's so bitter he's filled me full of lies and half truths about my mother. I've got to have some answers, Gabe. I can't go on wondering anymore."

"I don't much blame you," Gabe said gently, "but this isn't exactly the right time to go looking for anyone. Especially not in the Thicket."

"It's the right time for me," Elaine said.

Gabe looked at her. Something seemed to change in her eyes. It was a subtle shift of light, a sense of hunger and despair that reached out and drew him in.

Without taking her eyes off Gabe, Elaine stood and faced him. Her fingers loosed the top button of her shirt and slowly worked their way down. In a moment, Gabe could see a line of pale flesh down to her waist.

"I promised you there'd be a lot more," Elaine said, the words catching in her throat. "It's time I made good on that, Gabe."

Elaine slipped the shirt off her shoulders.

Gabe held his breath. "If this is in the way of a bribe, I got to tell you fair it won't work, Elaine. It'll be pure pleasure, that's for sure, but I won't take you into that swamp."

"Lord, Gabe, I don't care if you do or not," Elaine sighed. "It's the pleasure part I'm thinking on now!"

CHAPTER TWELVE

In the early morning darkness Elaine got out of bed, and Gabe helped her get dressed. The process took some time, allowing for kisses and touches here and there. More than once, the two were in danger of making their way back to the bed. Elaine was more than ready, but held Gabe off against her will.

"I have to get back," she insisted. "Honestly, Gabe, it's late enough as it is—or early, if you like. You want me to be walking out of the Excelsior Hotel in broad daylight? Why, anyone could tell by looking what I've been up to all night."

"It shows, all right," Gabe said.

"I'll say it does," Elaine sighed.

Gabe kissed her soundly at the door, and Elaine slipped off down the darkened hall. He waited until she was completely out of sight, then made his way back to the bed.

"Some kind of woman, all right," he said aloud. "Damned if she's not."

Gabe stretched out naked and put his hands behind his head. The first faint hint of false dawn crept in to lighten the shadows of the room. Gabe closed his eyes and grinned. He began to

recall the memories of the night, right from the beginning, when Elaine stood before him, touching the top button of her shirt. Every touch and every taste came to mind, and Gabe found it all just as wondrous as the first time around.

Gabe sat up and stared. The harsh light of noon filled the room. Someone pounded hard on the door. Gabe blinked and cursed beneath his breath. His feet found the floor, and he peered about the room for his pants. Suddenly, the wooden panels of the door burst into splinters; the bottom hinge snapped in half, and the door hung crookedly from the wall.

Jake Harper stalked in, stopped at the foot of Gabe's bed, and aimed his pistol at a spot between Gabe's eyes.

"Move, you son of a bitch," Harper said. "Just move a damn inch, and I'll gladly take off your head!"

Gabe froze. The gun trembled in Harper's hand, and the cold, unreasoning fury in his eyes told Gabe the man meant exactly what he said.

"I'm not moving," Gabe said evenly, "all right? You mind telling me what the hell this is all about?"

"You know damn well what it's about, you bastard," Harper said, the words catching in his throat. "It's about rape, mister, and by God it's going to give me pleasure to see your sorry neck danglin' from a rope!"

Gabe felt a sudden chill at the base of his spine. Harper's expression told him all he needed to know. The sheriff was dead serious, and he was itching to pull the trigger. All Gabe had to do was give him any small part of an excuse.

"Sheriff," Gabe said, bringing all the calm to his voice that he could muster, "I've been in this room all night. I haven't gone out. And I damn sure haven't ever raped a woman in my life. I never even—"

He saw Harper move and knew there wasn't any place to hide. The barrel of the pistol caught him square across the brow. Pain hit him hard, and everything came loose. He slid to the floor, grabbing helplessly for the edge of the bed.

"Get your pants on, you bastard!" Harper yelled. "Get on your feet!"

The words came from somewhere far away. Gabe pulled

himself to his knees, glanced up bleary-eyed, and tried to see the sheriff. There were two or three Harpers, and each of them had a gun.

"Leave me alone," Gabe said, "or go on and get it over with."

"I'm awful tempted, mister," Harper said. "Damned if I'm not."

Everything looked blurry and dark. Gabe heard the hammer click back and felt the cold muzzle between his eyes.

When Gabe came to and opened his eyes, he quickly shut them tight again. Seeing wasn't a good idea. Not yet. Not while the demons were hammering away inside his head.

When he woke up again, the ceiling had stopped oozing down the wall. He didn't have to guess where he was. The sour smell of urine and sweat told him that. Gritting his teeth he sat up, squinting against the pain.

"Couple of days, you'll be wishing I'd shot you on the spot," Harper said. "They tell me a rope ain't a pleasant way to go."

Gabe blinked, glanced up, and saw Harper standing before the bars of his cell.

"Why didn't you?" Gabe said. "Nobody'd ever know but you."

"Guess I wanted to string out the pleasure," Harper said. He gripped the bars and his face went hard as stone. "By God, I never much liked you, Conrad, but I'd never have figured you for this."

"Sheriff—"

"Shut your mouth!" Harper raged. His hand trembled as he drew a folded piece of paper from his pocket and tossed it at Gabe's feet.

"Read it," he snapped. "You got a legal right to do that. You want a lawyer, I'll try and get you one. Though I sure as hell don't know who'd want to take your case."

Harper turned and stalked off. Gabe heard a door slam down the hall, then he leaned down and picked up the paper. It read:

Snaketown

JEFFERSON, TEXAS
MARION COUNTY
NAME: Gabe Conrad
CHARGE: Rape and Assault
PLAINTIFF: Miss Elaine Porter
STATEMENT: On this date, I, Elaine Porter of Jefferson, Texas, do charge that Gabe Conrad did commit the crime of rape and assault against my person. Late in the evening last night, I went to Mr. Conrad's room in the Excelsior Hotel. The purpose of my visit was to bring Mr. Conrad an urgent message from my father, Mr. Robert Porter. I could see that Mr. Conrad was in a highly disturbed state of mind. He began taunting me at once, using foul language and suggestive talk. When I attempted to leave, Mr. Conrad brutally assaulted me and proceeded to rape me. Immediately after this event, I feigned unconsciousness, and, when Mr. Conrad left the room, I managed to escape. I wandered the streets for some time, unable to think clearly. Finally, I was able to inform a law enforcement officer in the person of Sheriff Jake Harper of this crime. I swear that the above is a true and accurate account.
Signed,
Elaine Porter
Witnessed by J. Harper, Sheriff, Jefferson, Texas.

Gabe stared at the paper, hoping that the words might disappear. Something was sure as hell wrong, he knew that. Elaine wouldn't pull something like this; he was certain. By God, she'd come up there on purpose, wanting the loving between them as much as he did.

Gabe cursed himself and crushed the paper in his hand. This had to do with his refusal to take her to the Thicket. It couldn't be anything else. Still, he couldn't believe she'd put his neck in a noose for just that. Get real mad at him, fine, he wouldn't be real surprised at that. But a hanging for rape . . .

He leaned back against the cold wall and closed his eyes. He had never shared a night with a woman who'd given herself

more freely and taken as much as she gave. Now it looked as if she had more to give than he'd ever counted on.

Gabe figured it was late afternoon. The sky outside his window was liquid brass. The air in his cell was foul and choking hot. A deputy brought a cup of stale water and left it within his reach. Gabe asked the man if he could get something to eat. The deputy told him no. He said the sheriff had informed him the prisoner had eaten a fine meal the night before last and wouldn't likely be hungry for a while.

Sounds like Harper, all right, Gabe thought grimly. That would be the sheriff's idea of a laugh. A roach crawled up the wall. It stopped to suck moisture from the stone and lurched drunkenly away. Gabe drank the last of his warm water and peered out the window of his cell. The solid brick wall of a warehouse blocked his view. A crow squawked somewhere out of sight. Someone down the hall shouted something he couldn't make out. More yelling and shouting followed that. A deputy ran past his cell and slammed a door. Then it was quiet again. Gabe pressed his face against the bars and tried to see down the hall. Now what the hell was that all about?

A door to his right opened quickly, and a black man in overalls came into Gabe's view. The man stopped and grinned at Gabe.

"You got a nasty cut there, Mr. Conrad," he said. "Ought to do something for it 'fore it gets infected real bad."

Gabe stared. "Who the hell are you? I don't—hey, I've seen you before. You drive the Porters' carriage. I saw you two nights ago."

"Sure did. The name's John Marshall." Marshall pulled a small piece of metal from his pocket, squinted at it in the light, and started to work on the lock of Gabe's cell, whistling to himself.

Gabe blinked. "What are you doing?"

"Just what it looks like, Mr. Conrad. Getting you out of this place."

Gabe watched Marshall work. "You're real handy with that."

"Guess I am. Wasn't born drivin' carriages around. Did a

Snaketown

little stealing 'fore that." He paused, spat on his hands, and tried again.

"Where'd everybody go?" Gabe asked. "You better hurry with that, before someone comes back."

Marshall didn't look up. "They'll be busy for a while. Right now they're trying to stop a bunch of fellas from robbin' the bank."

"Someone's robbing the bank?"

Marshall winked. "Sheriff thinks they are. Leastways, that's what I told him."

Something clicked in the lock. Marshall smiled, and opened the cell door. "Not much of a lock," he said scornfully. "They make 'em some better now. Best we be going, Mr. Conrad. I'd say we use the back door."

Gabe kept his questions to himself. He followed Marshall outside, past the brick building and into a tangle of brush and trees. A few yards further, he saw the two mounts tied to a tree.

"You take the gray," Marshall said. "The mare's used to me." He stopped and glanced at Gabe. "We could stand here and talk, and I could tell you what it is you want to know. Or we could get ourselves riding right quick. Ridin' seems the best idea to me."

"Sounds like good advice," Gabe said.

"Sure glad you see it that way," Marshall grinned. He mounted the mare, slapped the reins once and disappeared through the brush.

Marshall rode them hard southeast. In less than an hour, they had bypassed Marshall, Texas. Gabe's new friend said that's where he'd gotten his name. About an hour before sunset Marshall led them to a poor dirt farm on the edge of a dry creek. The horses were lathered and ready to drop. A weathered shack stood next to a corn-stubble field, and past that was a barn and a corral.

Marshall jumped down quickly and led the tired mounts to the barn. Two black men ran from the house and joined him. They didn't look at Gabe. Inside the barn were two fresh horses. One look at the fine, chestnut mounts told Gabe they

were as good as you could get, likely worth the price of the dreary piece of land where they'd stopped.

With the saddles in place, Gabe and Marshall were off again in less than five minutes. Not a word had passed between the three black men. It was clear that everyone knew exactly what to do, that the horses were there because that was exactly where they were supposed to be. Marshall explained nothing to Gabe, and Gabe kept his peace. He knew John Marshall was right. Talking had its place, and it came in a poor second now.

Gabe guessed it was nearly ten o'clock when Marshall raised his hand to stop. They were in a narrow valley of brush and scrub oak. A dark line of trees loomed off to the left, against the night sky. Marshall lit a match, let it burn, and blew it out. In a moment he struck another and blew that one out, too. Seconds later, a lantern blinked twice among the trees.

Marshall nodded to himself and told Gabe to leave the mounts where they were. Someone would be along to take them. Gabe followed Marshall through the brush across an open field.

"Mind if I ask where we are?" Gabe said. "I'd kind of like to know."

"You're a little east of Carthage, Texas," Marshall said. " 'Bout seven miles to be exact."

"Never heard of it."

"Ain't missed much, either."

Closer to the trees, Gabe saw a small camp fire burning in a shallow ravine. A shadow passed before the fire and came toward him, climbing up a slight rise. Elaine ran the last few yards, laughed, and fell into Gabe's arms.

"Oh, Gabe, I'm so glad to see you!" she said. "Lord, you must be plain exhausted." She pulled away and looked at Marshall. "Everything all right, John? Didn't have any trouble, I hope."

"Everything's fine, Miss Elaine. Didn't have any trouble at all."

Marshall walked off toward the fire. Gabe gripped Elaine's shoulders and held her out stiffly at arm's length.

"What's this I'm so glad to see you stuff?" he said harshly.

"Why'd you do it, Elaine? What the hell's going on here?"

"Gabe." Elaine made a face and squirmed out of his grip. "Is that any way to act? Honestly, you'd think a person would be somewhat grateful, us breaking you out of jail and all."

"Damn it all, woman, you're the one who put me in there. Am I supposed to be grateful for that?"

"For heaven's sake, Gabe." Elaine folded her arms and looked him squarely in the eye. "I had to do that. You said you wouldn't take me with you. I mean, it isn't like I didn't ask nice. I thought to myself, Elaine, what are you going to do with that man? Why, I'll give him some incentive, is what I'll do. If he doesn't have anywhere else to go, he'll feel more kindly toward going somewhere with me."

Gabe let out a breath. "I don't believe this, Elaine. I knew it had to be you when John Marshall showed up. But I sure didn't figure you'd have the gall to try and pull this. For God's sake, Elaine, you've put me on the run. By now every lawman in the state knows it's perfectly all right to shoot Gabe Conrad on sight!"

"Oh, but they won't," Elaine protested. "Because I'll tell them that I lied, Gabe. My heavens, there wasn't any rape. I'd say it was *somewhat* more enjoyable than that."

"Thanks. I'm sure glad to hear it."

"I'm only saying what I feel, Gabe." She came to Gabe again, stretching out her hands.

"Forget it, Elaine." Gabe shook his head. "You've given me a hell of a bump on the head and wasted a lot of time. I'd rather be on the run than take you into some swamp. Hell, I'd rather hide out in Mexico."

"Oh you would, would you?" Elaine stuck out her chin in defiance. "Well, you just go to Mexico, Gabe Conrad. It's a real long hike so you better get started right now 'cause I haven't got a horse I can spare."

Elaine turned and stomped off toward the fire. Gabe watched her go.

"I'm damned if I'll let you get away with this, woman," he muttered to himself. "But I got to have something to eat, there isn't any way around that."

CHAPTER THIRTEEN

Gabe woke to the smell of frying fish. The sky was still dark in the west, but Marshall had somehow managed to catch four large perch, set them sizzling in cornmeal and fat, and get the coffee on.

Shaking off sleep, Gabe stood and stretched. He tried to ignore the dull pounding in his head, a reminder of the way Jake Harper had greeted him the morning before. Yesterday seemed a long time ago. Time had a way of lazing on or winking by, depending on how much aggravation you had to shovel through that day.

Frowning at the taste in his mouth, Gabe stumbled to the fire and poured himself a scalding cup.

"Too early for morning, you ask me," he said. "Ought to have it later in the day."

Marshall looked up from his chores. "I see we ain't waking up real pleasant like. I guess you didn't sleep too fine."

"I did the best I could. Where's the lady of the house? She out taking a carriage ride or what?"

"Down by the creek washing up."

"You didn't bring a tub along? I'm sure surprised to hear that. Looks to me like you got about everything else."

Marshall grinned. "Miss Elaine, she likes to do things right." He nodded toward the gear stacked neatly by a large oak tree. "All your stuff's over there. Got it out of your hotel room 'fore we left. Your weapon and all your belongings. Everything's there."

Gabe raised a brow. "Well, I'll be damned."

"Like I say—"

"Yeah, I know. Miss Elaine likes to do things right."

Elaine walked up the hill, looking pretty and fresh in clean jeans and a checkered shirt, her dark hair sparkling in the first rays of the sun. Gabe tried to think about the fool stunt she'd pulled, how she'd suckered him in and put every lawman in Texas on his tail. He tried to keep thinking of how mad he was at this girl, instead of the way she looked.

"Morning," Elaine said brightly. "My, that fish smells delicious, John."

Elaine sat down and crossed her legs, found herself a plate, and helped herself to the fish.

"Hope you slept well, Gabe," she said. "I just dropped right off. I love to camp outdoors."

Gabe set down his plate. "Elaine, I don't want to talk about how nice everybody slept and what a fine day it is. What I want to talk about is what I'm going to do next. Which is leave and get as far away from Texas as I can. And I don't intend to walk, so don't get started on that."

Elaine shrugged. "I hope you won't do that, Gabe."

"Well, hope all you want. That's the way it's going to be."

Gabe stood and stabbed a finger at Elaine. "In the first place, you haven't worked all this out as well as you think. Jake Harper's not stupid. How long you think it'll take for him to figure this out? John Marshall works for you, and he gets me out of jail. Suddenly, you're out of town. Harper'll know what happened in about two minutes flat."

"I doubt that's the way it'll be," Elaine said. "You see, before John left he sorta confided in a friend that he *had* to let you out. 'Cause your confederates had kidnapped me, and they'd do me bodily harm if he didn't go along. This friend of John's has told this all to Jake by now. So—"

"Confederates!" Gabe looked at Elaine and glared at Marshall. Marshall found something interesting to see down the hill. "And you think Harper'll buy that?"

"Well, of course he will, Gabe." Elaine gave him her very best innocent look. "Jake is certainly not going to think I'd ride off with you. He wouldn't let himself believe an awful thing like that."

Gabe let out a breath. "How did I get myself tangled up in a mess like this?"

"Gabe. Sit down and talk to me, will you?"

"I don't want to sit down."

"Well, do it anyway, all right?"

Gabe sat. He threw his coffee in the fire; the flames hissed and threw a gust of steam toward the sky.

"I don't want to hear about how you think you've got to find your mother," Gabe said. "If you want to, that's fine. I don't blame you for that. But this running off into who knows how many miles of the Thicket isn't going to get you what you want. You think she's in there, or she might be in there, but you don't know, Elaine. You're just going to wander around and get lost."

Elaine leaned forward and gripped Gabe's hand in both of hers. "I won't get lost, Gabe. And I know my mother's in there because—" Elaine looked away and bit her lip. "Because John's been bringing me letters from my mother for nearly a year now. This is not a fool's errand like you think. She knows I'm coming, Gabe."

Gabe stared. "You didn't tell me any of this before. All I heard was how Old Jim took you fishing and told you all about the swamp. Old Jim, my foot."

"Well, there *was* an Old Jim," Elaine pouted. "Only, he didn't exactly take me fishing anywhere. Gabe, I didn't tell you everything because I didn't think you'd believe me. Anyway, you said you wouldn't go with me, so I didn't see much reason to tell you more. I'm sorry, all right? I did what I thought I had to do. Maybe I should have tried another way."

Gabe looked curiously at Elaine. "If you know where your mother is, what do you need me for? Why'd you have to go through all this? You and Marshall can just—"

"I said I knew she was *in* there, Gabe. I didn't say I knew where she was. She leaves letters for me in a stump, and John picks them up. She knows I'm going to come to her, but we've got to go in first. The people in the Thicket are very careful. Remember? You told me that, and you're right. They don't care for strangers. We have to go in, and let my mother find *us*. We'll see somebody, I know."

"Or somebody'll find us," Gabe finished. "And not necessarily your mother's people. All right, that's what you want with me. Miss Elaine's hired gun."

"Gabe, that's not true," Elaine protested. "I need you, yes, but I also want you with me. Because I just do. Do I have to remind you about . . ." Elaine blushed. "Well, do I?"

"Yeah, fine," Gabe said, wondering just what he could believe anymore. "Let's forget about the Thicket for a minute. There's something else, Elaine. You may not think it's real important, but I sure as hell do. A lot's happened in Jefferson the last couple of days. There are three people dead. That Holzer fellow tried to gun me down. Something's going on, and I don't know what it is. Maybe you've got an idea; I don't know. If you don't, your father sure does."

Elaine's face went slack. "I don't know what you're talking about. You don't have any business bringing my father into those horrible things that happened. Or me either!"

Elaine tried to control her emotions, but it was clear she was shaken by his words.

"You know what I'm talking about, Elaine," Gabe said. "Even your friend Jake Harper knows things don't just happen like they did. Caddo Jack's in this mess somewhere, but someone else is, too. You can run off to the swamp, but you can't leave trouble behind. It'll catch up with you sure as the sun comes up."

Elaine stood and nervously brushed her hands against her jeans. "John, we've got a long day's ride," she said. "I think we should get things packed and underway. Gabe, are you coming or not? Do what you want. It makes no difference to me."

"I don't see I have a lot of choice," Gabe said. "If I don't see that you get back safe, I'll be running around with a price on my head, and I'm not too excited about that."

"Fine," Elaine said coolly, "I'm pleased that you see things my way."

Gabe watched her as she walked down the hill toward the horses, standing tall and proud like a woman who was used to things going her way.

Gabe, Elaine, and Marshall broke camp early Wednesday morning. Marshall set a hard pace, leading them steadily to the south. Gabe waited for a noontime break, but Marshall didn't stop.

Just as Gabe was certain the mounts would drop dead in their tracks, a copse of trees would appear, or a run-down barn, and there would be a black man or two with fresh horses, ready for the next leg of the trip.

Gabe had often heard the saying that money talks, and now he saw that it did. Elaine had wired ahead where the telegraph ran and sent out riders where it didn't. She had quickly organized her own Pony Express; eveyone was where they were told to be and when. It irritated Gabe no end to see Elaine remain totally calm throughout the trip. She was confident that everything would happen exactly as she'd planned.

Gabe wasn't all that sure. Other people could ride a horse, and they knew about the telegraph, too. He was certain Jake Harper had spread the word to every lawman within two hundred miles of Jefferson. There were a lot of places to look, but it was only a matter of time before someone spotted three riders moving hard for the south.

It was Marshall who spotted the lawmen first. Late on Thursday afternoon, he raised his hand and brought Gabe and Elaine to a halt. Gabe rode up and saw ten or twelve horsemen half a mile off to the east.

"They're after us, sure as hell," Gabe said.

"Appears that they are," Marshall said. He glanced at Elaine. "We can sit here and wait. They're heading away, and they ain't going to see us. Only thing is, they keep going the way they are, they're likely going to pick up our tracks going south."

"We'll wait for a minute," Elaine said impatiently. "It's clear they haven't seen us, and I doubt they'll find our trail."

"You're real sure of that, are you?" Gabe said.

"Why, yes, Gabe, I am. Come on, John, we're wasting precious time."

Elaine kicked her mount soundly and bounded off ahead. Gabe shook his head. They had avoided each other since Wednesday morning and scarcely exchanged a dozen words. The temperature was in the high nineties somewhere, but the hard chill between them showed no indication of thawing out.

Marshall seemed to guess his thoughts. "Miss Elaine, she got a way about her, that's for sure."

"She's a number one pain in the ass is what she is," Gabe muttered to himself.

The land had been changing since the second day out. Scrub oak and brush gave way to hardwood and pine, and, by Friday morning, a whole new world began to appear. The three riders passed Big Sandy Creek in the late afternoon. Three hours after that, the first of the Thicket's swampland appeared. The humid air was a nearly visible pall. The woods were thick with white oak and tupelo. Giant cypress trees shaded the dark bayou waters. There were wild azaleas about, swamp buttercups, and a thousand shades of green. Cottonmouths twisted through the waters, and a lone blue heron stood watch from a fallen log.

A black man Gabe guessed to be a hundred years old was waiting in a grove of willows by a flat-bottomed boat. John Marshall greeted the man. Elaine spoke to him for a moment, then turned to Gabe.

"Well, we're here," she said evenly, "just like I told you, Gabe."

"We're somewhere," Gabe said sullenly. "I'm not real sure I know where."

Elaine looked at him a long moment. Then, her expression seemed to soften and she smiled. "Do we have to keep acting like this?" she said gently. "We didn't start out this way."

"I know how we started out," Gabe said.

"You think we could maybe go back and start over? I'm sorry for what I did. I already told you that."

"I know you did."

"And you're not about to forgive me for that."

Gabe didn't answer. The words he wanted to say were there, but he couldn't get them out.

Elaine watched him, the color rising to her face. "Then you can go to hell," she said softly. "I have done all the apologizing I care to do."

She turned away quickly and walked back to the edge of the bayou. "Get everything in the boat if you will, John. Isn't any reason we're standing around here."

Gabe picked up his gear. Looking out over the swamp, he saw a flash of red among the trees. Then, a pair of large red birds took wing and disappeared off to the west.

"Glad to see something knows where it's going," he muttered to himself. "That makes two of you."

CHAPTER FOURTEEN

Since it was nearly six o'clock, Gabe suggested they camp on shore for the night and get an early start the next day. Elaine refused to listen. They were *there*, and there was no use wasting time. Marshall's expression indicated that he knew Gabe was right, but he didn't say a word. He simply nodded and loaded up the boat. A few moments later, they left dry land behind.

Almost at once, the boat was swallowed in a hot and humid world. Dense growth closed in around them in a tangle of big-boled cypress and choking vines. Green palmetto fronds masked their way on either side. The sluggish water was mirror black, cut off from the light overhead. When the day managed to pierce the thick canopy above, it struck the water in muted shafts of yellow-green, as if the sun had passed through dirty panes of glass.

Gabe had known misery before, but the Thicket set new standards for discomfort and heat. Not a breeze stirred. The air was almost too thick to breathe. Dark clots of mosquitoes settled in about the boat, looking for places to hide in noses and eyes. Every time Gabe opened his mouth, a dozen whining bugs fought to get in. Marshall had brought a cure, a concoc-

tion of rancid fish oil. The stuff smelled awful, but it kept the mosquitoes away.

Moments before the night closed in, Marshall found a partially dry hammock of land and pulled ashore without consulting Elaine. A giant cypress tree loomed over this narrow patch of earth; Spanish moss bearded its branches, reaching nearly to the surface of the water.

Gabe wondered if they'd gone half a mile. If Marshall's compass hadn't pointed due south, he would have sworn they were back where they'd begun.

Elaine seemed perfectly satisfied. She acted as if she knew exactly where she was.

"Well, we made a little progress," she said. "I think we're off to a real fine start."

"Finest place I've ever been," Gabe said, earning a scathing look from Elaine.

Marshall had shot a few squirrels just before they reached the swamp. He wrapped the meat in green leaves and cooked it on a forked stick under a thick slice of fatback. While the squirrels cooked, he made a soup of wild onions and potatoes, tossing in some peppercorns and salt. The meal was complete with small rolls, dough pinched off a ball, wrapped around a stick, and turned over the fire.

Gabe told Marshall it was the finest meal he'd ever had, even better than his feast at the Excelsior Hotel. Marshall beamed and said it was likely a whole lot cheaper as well.

"John likes you, Gabe," Elaine said later, joining Gabe by the fire. "He doesn't care for a lot of white folks. For good reason, I suppose."

"You treat a man with respect, he'll likely give it back," Gabe said.

Elaine let out a breath and pushed a strand of hair from her cheek. "I guess that was kind of meant for me. What I did, it didn't show much respect for you, I don't guess."

"That's over and done with now."

"Is it?" Elaine looked at him.

"I'd like it to be," Gabe said honestly. He had known all along that he couldn't stay angry with Elaine and was glad

she'd given him the chance to say it. "I don't see any reason for you and me to be at odds. More good's happened between us than bad."

"I'd say it has, all right." She looked down at her hands. "Maybe that means we might stay on the same side of the fire tonight."

Elaine glanced up at him, and Gabe saw a familiar secret smile, a flash of excitement in her eyes. He nodded across the fire at John Marshall. "Sounds fine to me, but we've sorta got company, Elaine."

"John's a pretty smart man," Elaine said. "I expect he'll figure that if you and me are talking again, he might ought to bed down somewhere on the far end of this piece of land."

"I expect he'll do just that. Like you say, John's a pretty wise fellow."

Gabe added a few sticks of their sparse supply of dry kindling to the fire and pulled his pack further back beneath the big cypress tree. While he struggled with his boots, Elaine spread her blanket on the ground.

"Honestly, Gabe, I don't think you're going to need *this* tonight. Not 'less you think a blizzard's going to blow through the swamp."

Gabe turned and saw she was holding up a long coat from his pack. "I'd say you're right," he told her. "I doubt we're going to get real cold."

Elaine studied the garment with a curious eye. "I don't think I've ever seen anything like it," she said. "Is it—buffalo?"

Gabe looked soberly at the well-worn coat of buffalo hide, at the faint yellow outline of the Indian Thunderbird painted on the back.

"Yes, it's buffalo," he said finally.

Elaine caught the sound of his voice. "It's important to you, isn't it? I've never seen that look on your face before."

"It means something to me."

"And I don't have any business asking what, right? I'm sorry, I didn't mean to pry."

"You're not prying," Gabe said. "The coat was—it comes from my mother's tipi, Elaine. That symbol, the bird there, is

Wakinyan, the Thunderbird. She painted it there—some time before she died."

Elaine looked puzzled. "You're Indian, Gabe? I didn't know, 'cause you don't look—"

"I'm not," Gabe said. "My mother and father were settlers. The Sioux attacked their wagon train in the Black Hills. My father was killed, and one of the braves took my mother to live in his camp. She was pregnant with me. When I was born, my mother decided to raise me as a Sioux. She didn't have much choice. I was a Lakota till I was about fifteen, and then she sent me to live with the whites."

Elaine studied her hands. "That must have been a hard thing for her to do."

"It was," Gabe said. "I didn't understand it for a long time, what she did. She knew what was going to happen to the Indians in this country. She knew I'd have a chance to make it in the white world. She wanted to give me that chance."

"And now she's gone."

"She's dead," Gabe said harshly. He looked past Elaine into the dark. "They killed her. Cavalry troops rode down on her village and slaughtered everyone there."

"Oh, Gabe."

"It's all done. It's past."

"I don't think that's true. I don't think it'll ever be all done with you."

Gabe knew she was right. It was over, but it would never be finished. Not in his heart. He had buried her after the battle, scooping out a grave in the hard ground, then covering the site with dirt and stones. Later, he had tracked down the U. S. Cavalry captain who had murdered his mother, and wreaked his revenge.

He didn't tell that part to Elaine. The fact that he had told her as much as he did came as a surprise to Gabe. The part of him that would always be Long Rider of the Lakota kept his secrets to himself. Still, it was Gabe who sat next to Elaine by a fire in the Thicket, and Gabe who felt it was good to have someone close to him on that particular night.

Their lovemaking in the Excelsior Hotel had been fierce and demanding. This time, they knew each other well and there was

nothing they had to prove. After they had satisfied each other, Elaine sighed, and Gabe dropped down beside her, breathing in great gulps of air.

"I don't guess we're mad at each other anymore," Elaine whispered. "Least that's the way it felt to me."

"If that's being mad," Gabe said, "I'd as soon stay angry all the time."

"I don't think we have to do that anymore," Elaine said, and Gabe silently agreed.

Breakfast was catfish cooked in cornmeal and coarse black pepper. Gabe and Elaine wolfed down their portions as quickly as Marshall could bring them from the pan. Marshall didn't wonder what had caused such voracious appetites. He had moved his bed far away from the fire the night before, but he wasn't stone deaf. At breakfast, he did his best to keep a solemn face and quickly found chores to handle by the boat.

The swamp was covered by a heavy fog until an hour past sunrise. Elaine decided it was prudent to wait until they could see at least a foot or two ahead. When they finally got underway again, they found the dark water ahead thick with swamp grass and second growth willow. Once, they rowed up a narrow creek choked with vines and rotting logs. The creek ended abruptly, and it took a good hour tracking back.

Gabe saw Elaine had lost some of her confidence from the day before. She looked warily to the left and to the right, nervously biting her lip and running a hand across her throat. Finally, she told Marshall she wasn't sure he'd launched their boat from the right spot.

"I got the right place, Miss Elaine," Marshall insisted. "Ain't no mistake about that."

"What place are we talking about?" Gabe said.

"The spot where John has picked up letters from my mother and left notes of mine," Elaine explained. "I told you about that. She had a stump we used. I just thought that maybe John had gotten the wrong stump. I mean, they all look pretty much alike."

"Oh, that's good," Gabe said.

"Got the very same stump," Marshall said evenly. "I can

tell one stump from the next, I reckon."

"I'm sure I'm wrong then," said Elaine.

"Yes, ma'am. I got to say you are."

A trail of the morning's fog still clung to the darker backwaters of the swamp. By noon the sun began to bake the earth, and the last cloudy veil disappeared, baring a ghostly forest of dead and bearded pines. It looked to Gabe like the graveyard of a thousand wrecked ships, their stark masts etched against a brassy sky.

Marshall pulled under a thick stand of Spanish moss and passed out dried meat and bread for lunch. The gnats came in swarms to the feast, but there was nothing to be done about that. Gabe saw a red bird take flight, the same kind he'd seen just before they took to the swamp. It was as big as a hawk, with jet and white feathers and a startling crest of red.

"Ivory-billed woodpecker," Marshall told him. "See 'em all over the place."

"Size of that thing," Gabe said, "it's a wonder there's any trees left."

"Plenty of trees," Marshall said. "Take a lot of those birds to—"

"John!" Elaine waved him quickly into silence. Gabe looked at her. There was fear in her eyes; the skin was stretched tightly across her face.

Elaine pointed through the hanging moss toward the rise of dry land across the swamp. Gabe spread the moss cautiously with his hands. A line of riders poked their way through the brush, heading roughly southwest on a course parallel with their own, scarcely fifty yards away. Fifteen, twenty, twenty-five of them, Gabe counted. None of the men spoke a word, and each one carried a Winchester rifle across his saddle.

"Oh my God!" Elaine suddenly drew in a breath and tightened her fingers on Gabe's arm. Gabe looked closer and saw what had drawn an exclamation from Elaine. Robert Porter was leading the pack. He rode a fine black gelding, gripping the reins with one hand and holding a rifle tightly with the other.

"He knows," Elaine said, and Gabe could hear the tremor in her voice. "He know's my mother's in here, too."

CHAPTER FIFTEEN

Gabe reached over and touched Elaine's cheek, turning her face to meet his own. "You don't have a reason in the world to think that. He's looking for you and me is what he's doing. That doesn't surprise me at all."

"No." Elaine shook her head, her gaze still locked on the scene across the swamp. "I can't say how I know, but I do. I can feel it, Gabe. Like something real cold touched my back. He knows she's in here. It isn't just me!"

Gabe didn't argue. Marshall looked curiously at Elaine, then turned away. Whatever he was thinking, he kept it to himself.

Marshall waited a long time until he was certain the riders were past. After a whispered conference with Gabe, the two decided to bear southeast to put distance between themselves and the riders. There was always the danger of meeting them again, but the only other option was north, the way they'd come, and they knew Elaine would never consider turning back.

After the encounter with her father's riders, Elaine barely spoke two words. Some demon of the past had reached out and touched her, thrust her into silence. Gabe knew it was useless

to try to help. Whatever had taken her would eventually let her go; nothing he could say would bring her back until she was ready to make the trip.

Gabe lost all track of time. His childhood among the Lakota had given him a keen sense of the passage of day and night, but that sense seemed next to useless in the Thicket. Here, sun and shadow played tricks on the eye, masking the hours in tangled growth and water that swallowed the light.

Every time Gabe got used to his surroundings, the scenery began to change. Without warning, the thick canopy of bearded cypress gave way to open water the color of slate. The tip of Gabe's oar told him the muddy bottom was only inches below the surface.

"We're going to have to cross over in the open," Marshall said. "I'm not too happy 'bout that."

"We can't stay here," Gabe agreed. "Just stay as close to shore as you can."

Marshall nodded, and they set out cautiously, using the sparse cover of skeletal trees as best they could. The shore of the flat marshland was dotted with yellow irises. Ahead and to the left was a tangle of willow and sharp-leaved holly. Farther, Gabe could see the willows gave way to a steep hammock of pine and the promise of welcome shade. If we can make it to the trees, Gabe thought, get the boat in good cover again . . .

Gabe froze as a man suddenly appeared, standing less than ten feet away. A second before there was nothing but swamp grass ahead, and then the man was there, seemingly rising out of nowhere, a long Sharps rifle older than Gabe trained on the boat.

"Afternoon, folks," the man said. "Sure a fine day for a boat ride, ain't it?"

Gabe heard Elaine draw in a breath. Marshall's hand inched for the shotgun, but Gabe shook his head and warned him off.

The man took in this silent exchange and rewarded them with a gap-toothed grin. "Sound thinking, mister."

"We're not looking for any trouble," Gabe said. He wondered if he could get to the Colt before the man could fire

the rifle and knew it would be a dead heat. He'd likely get the man, but one of them would die, too.

"I'm right relieved to hear that," the man said evenly. "I ain't lookin' for none either. What you folks doin' out here? You git lost or what?" The question was addressed to Gabe, but the man's eyes constantly flicked to Elaine.

Before Gabe could answer, the swamp grass parted, and Gabe saw the man was standing in a boat. A younger man was at the oars. The men seemed cast from the same mold. They were gaunt, bearded men in patched cotton trousers and calico shirts faded by too many washings. Each wore a tattered straw hat.

"We're not lost," Gabe said, forcing an easy grin. "Just going over to visit a fellow."

The man raised a brow at that. "You got friends out here?"

Gabe had a tale all ready for the man, about a gator hunter he'd known for some years who'd invited him to come and visit. Elaine broke in before he could get the story out.

"We're looking for my mother," she said abruptly. "Her name is Lil. Maybe you know her, or where I could find her? I'd be grateful for your help."

Gabe wanted to strangle the girl, but it was too late for that.

"Don't recall I ever heard of the lady," the man said. His easy smile never changed, but Gabe could read the sudden interest in his eyes. " 'Course, don't guess I know everyone there is."

"Well, we thank you anyway," Gabe said. "Nice to meet you, mister. I reckon we'll be on our way."

"Now I don't guess you ought to do that," the man said. His smile faded at once, and his voice went deadly flat. "We'd take it kindly if you'd stop off and visit a spell. Think you might see your way to do that?"

Gabe searched the man's eyes and saw what was there. In the man's mind, he and John Marshall were no longer in the picture. And Elaine . . .

"I guess we could," Gabe said. "A chance to rest up wouldn't hurt."

"Gabe . . ."

"Take it easy," Gabe said. He didn't take his eyes off the man in the boat. "Everything will be fine. The man wants us to visit, why we will."

"Now that's a real sound decision," the man grinned. "Edgar, take us back down the draw. These folks will follow right behind."

The man eased himself down. The muzzle of his rifle never wavered from Gabe's chest. The Sharps was a Big Fifty, and it could throw lead for five miles. No one ever shot that far, of course—one or two hundred yards was a good enough range for buffalo. At ten or twelve feet, the bullet would tear Gabe apart, go clean through Marshall and Elaine, and bury itself in a tree a mile away.

The man had to know there were riders about; he wouldn't want to use the weapon, knowing it would bring unwanted attention to this part of the Thicket. He wouldn't want to shoot, but he would. He'd shoot, and then he'd disappear. The bodies would never be found, and that would be the end of that.

Before he let that happen, Gabe knew he'd have to get off a shot or two. They'd all three catch it, but Elaine would be better off dead than going off with this pair. At that moment, Elaine reached out and touched his hand. Her eyes told him she knew this as well.

Half an hour or so after the two boats left the marshy lake, they were once more swallowed up in shadow. There were low tussocks of land on either side. Gallberry bushes grew thick and over ten feet high. Black gum, water oak, and bay trees choked the way ahead. In spite of these dark and gloomy surroundings, bright flowers abounded everywhere. Hundreds of snow-colored and snakemouth orchids clung to the vines and trees. The air was heavy with the smell of mold. Gabe figured if you touched anything in here, it would fall apart with rot.

"Never seen a bay gall before, have you?" The man grinned. "Right pretty place to stink so damn much. Might be I ought to stop and pick the lady some flowers. What you think, Edgar?"

Edgar showed Elaine a vacant grin.

"Edgar'd like that," the man said. "I think he's taken a shine to you, gal."

"Listen—" Gabe began.

"You don't say nothing, mister," the man said flatly. "Isn't anything I want to hear from you."

The man glanced around, taking in his surroundings. "This here's as good a place as any," he told the younger man. "Pull over to that there dry piece of ground." He waved his rifle at Gabe and Marshall. "Both of you. Git out and stand over there. Go on, *move!*"

"No!" Elaine stared at the man. "You can't have—any reason to do us harm!"

"Isn't any *us*, gal," the man said. "You ain't in this at all."

"It's all right," Gabe said. He sent her a silent signal with his eyes. *I'll try*, the message said. *I'll do what I can.*

Gabe and Marshall stepped out of the boat. The land sank a good foot beneath their boots. Gabe glanced once at Elaine and looked away.

"Turn around," the man said. "I ain't lookin' to cause you pain. You likely won't feel a thing."

Gabe didn't move. Marshall let out a breath beside him.

"Suit yerself," the man said. "Edgar, use that pistol of yours on 'em. Push it in close in the gut, and it'll ease the sound some. Do the white feller first, then the—"

Gabe moved. His hand was a blur as he whipped the Colt from under his arm. The big barrel of the Sharps centered right on Gabe's belly. An instant after Gabe fired, he heard something like a bee drone past his head, then another after that.

The man stared out at nothing, and the Sharps fell from his hand. Gabe's shot had ruined his left eye; an arrow had struck him in the mouth and pierced the back of his head. He sat stiffly for a moment, then tumbled into the black water. Edgar sat very still, his head on his chest. A second arrow was buried in his heart.

Elaine cried out, and Gabe jerked around, the Colt still gripped in his hand.

"Don't go shootin' at me," a voice said. "I'm a friend."

"Come out and show yourself, friend," Gabe said sharply.

"I don't like to shake hands with anyone I can't see."

The thick vines behind Gabe parted. A towheaded young man wearing overalls and no shirt stepped out. His long hair was tied back with a string. He held a bow in one hand and grinned at Gabe.

"My name's Keetch," the man said. "Right pleased to meet you folks."

Gabe holstered his weapon and shook Keetch's hand. "Glad to see you, too. Don't guess I have to say that."

The young man grinned. "Been followin' you a spell. Just had to find the right time to introduce myself." He glanced at Edgar and the man floating face down nearby. "Bad luck, you meetin' up with them two. They's McCabes is who they are. Were. All the McCabes is flat mean, but that'n there was the worst. He's Amos McCabe. The younggun's his boy."

Gabe shook his head and looked at Keetch. "The last man I saw get two arrows off that fast was named Crooked Leg, and he was a Sioux. You're mighty handy with that."

Keetch shrugged. "You go after game in here with a gun, one of something's all yer goin' to git."

"We're grateful," said Elaine. "Those two—"

"They'd have done you right badly, ma'am," Keetch finished. "And your ma would've never forgive me for lettin' that happen."

"You—you know my mother?" Elaine's face lit up with joy. "Is that true, you know her?"

"Sure do," Keetch said. "She figured you'd be comin' along 'bout now."

"Please, tell me, is she—"

"Time for talk later," Keetch said. He turned to Gabe. "That shot of yours will carry pretty far. We better be headin' out now."

Keetch walked past Gabe, picked up the limp form of Edgar, and rolled him into the water. "Don't have to worry 'bout buryin' a feller out here. Gators and other critters'll take care of everything 'fore dark."

Gabe looked soberly at the two figures. It was a sorry way to go, but he felt no remorse for the McCabes. He and Marshall could've just as easily been floating face down in the swamp.

• • •

"Is it very much further?" Elaine asked. "Please, Keetch, just tell me is my mother all right? Is she well and everything? You must understand, it's been a long time and I'm quite anxious, you know?"

"I sure do understand," Keetch said. "Answer to yer first question, we're about ten minutes away. As to the second, your mother's just fine. Real anxious to see you, too."

"She knew we were coming, you said," Gabe asked. "How did she know that?"

"Didn't exactly *know*. But she figured that you'd come." Keetch's smile faded. "Weren't easy gettin' around out there today. Something's stirred up the place. There's riders to the east and west both. Mostly gettin' theyselves lost, but it's a pure aggravation if you're trying to stay out of sight." Keetch raised a questioning brow at Gabe and Elaine, as if they might shed some light on the business of the riders. No one volunteered, and Keetch let the question go.

Gabe, Marshall, and Elaine had followed Keetch's suggestion and left their own, somewhat smaller boat in the bay gall, in favor of Keetch's. Keetch assured them there were plenty of boats to be had where they were heading, and they could have their choice when they liked. Keetch's boat was long and narrow, more in the shape of a canoe, and Keetch seemed able to take it through any passage with a two-foot clearance and an inch or so of water.

Late in the afternoon, the land around them changed again. Dense, tangled growth gave way to dark water under the shade of thick-boled cypress trees. The boat seemed suspended in a cavern underground. There was relatively dry land on either side now; farther, through the cypress, Gabe could see willow and stunted oaks. A gray squirrel chattered above, sending a lark sparrow into flight.

Finally, Keetch let the boat drift up a narrow creek. Gabe smelled wood smoke and cooking meat. Through the trees, he caught sight of wooden shacks with roofs of dried palmetto fronds and a trace of split-rail fences sagging in every direction.

" 'Bout home," Keetch said. He rowed a few more strokes

and then reached out to grab the end of a narrow plank wharf. He steadied the boat while the others climbed out.

Elaine could scarcely contain herself. She bit her lip and grinned, taking in everything at once.

"Won't be long," Keetch told her. "Your mother's place is to the right off the path. You'll see it when we get through the trees."

"Oh, Gabe!" Elaine squeezed his arm. "You don't know what this means to me." She looked at Marshall. "You do, I know, John. I owe much of this to you."

"Didn't do anything at all," Marshall said. "Don't you go saying I did, Miss Elaine."

"Your mother's likely changed some," Gabe told her. "You know that."

"I'll remember her," Elaine said.

"Well, I guess you might."

"I know I will, Gabe. The years in between don't matter. I'll—"

Elaine stopped. A man stepped through the undergrowth ten feet away.

Gabe felt something hard knot up in his belly. They were here; everything was all right, and then suddenly, everything was terribly wrong, and he knew there was nothing he could do, no way to turn back.

"By God, Conrad, this sure is fine," Holzer said. "I can't think of anyone I'd rather have come visitin' than you."

CHAPTER SIXTEEN

"I've got to tell the truth," Gabe said. "There's two or three people I'd rather see than you. What the hell are you doing here, Holzer? They got a big poker game going in the swamp?"

Holzer laughed. "You got it, mister. And I've been savin' a place for you." Without warning, he drew his gun and aimed it at Gabe's head. "Keetch, you check these folks for guns? This feller's got a habit of keeping a Colt hid under his arm."

Keetch looked curiously at Holzer. "I knew they had some weapons. Didn't see no cause to take 'em away."

"Well do it now, damn you!" Holzer said angrily. "And check the nigger, too." He let his eyes roam over Elaine, pausing to take in the sights. "What about you, ma'am? You hidin' something I might ought to see?"

Elaine flushed. "Gabe, I've seen this man before. He came in on the *Cypress Moon* with you." Elaine paused and stared, as if she'd just caught Holzer's name. "Oh, Lord, that's him, isn't it?"

"That's the one," Gabe said. "He rode by a little too fast to say hello." Gabe held up his arms while Keetch jerked the gun from his shoulder holster. As Gabe glanced at Keetch's hands, Holzer took two quick steps and swung a big right fist.

Gabe looked up in time to see the blow coming. Holzer's

fist caught him on the side of the head and sent him sprawling. Gabe hit the ground hard, rolled, and came up to his knees. Holzer's boot caught him solidly in the ribs. Gabe swallowed the pain and threw himself aside. He kicked out blindly and felt the satisfying weight of a belly beneath his boot.

Holzer staggered back, grabbing at his gut. Gabe came off the ground and hit him solidly in the jaw. The blow was good enough to drop an ox, but Holzer was solid rock. He grinned and spit blood, shook his head and circled Gabe, big fists doubled before his face.

From the corner of his eye, Gabe saw a crowd had gathered to watch the show. A good fight usually brought yells and catcalls, shouts egging on one man or the other. These men simply watched. There was no expression at all in their thin and somber faces.

Gabe waited, watching Holzer move. Holzer's good hand was his right. He jabbed out now and then with the left, leaving himself open and inviting Gabe in. The next time Holzer lashed out, Gabe walked into the big right, ducked under Holzer's swing, and planted another belly punch. Holzer groaned and staggered back, arms flailing in the air.

Holzer's head was an open target, and Gabe moved in fast, ready to finish the man off. Suddenly, Holzer stopped, caught his balance, and slammed one foot against the ground. Gabe caught the man's grin and knew at once he'd been suckered in.

Holzer clamped his fists together and put his weight behind the blow. It caught Gabe's shoulder like a hammer. Gabe felt his left arm go numb. Holzer was all over him then, punishing him with short, cutting jabs aimed at tearing Gabe's face to a pulp. In desperation, Gabe grabbed a piece of Holzer's shirt, jerked him in close, and thrust his knee at Holzer's crotch. Holzer took the blow with his thigh, but the move was enough to turn his attention from Gabe's face. Gabe sent all the strength he could muster to his good right arm and smashed his fist into Holzer's nose.

Holzer howled. His eyes glazed, and he stumbled back. Gabe darted in close, lashing out at Holzer's head. Holzer raised his hands and fought back, driving Gabe away. Gabe

cursed and backed off, amazed that Holzer was still on his feet. He wondered what the hell it would take to bring this big bastard down. Holzer was swaying, shaking the cobwebs out of his head, but he was still on his feet.

Gabe circled the man warily, looking for an opening. He knew what one blow of those ham-sized fists could do and didn't care to meet one again. The feeling was returning to his arm, but it wouldn't do a whole lot of damage for a while, and Holzer likely knew that, too.

Gabe came in close, feinting with his left, daring Holzer to lash out again. Holzer wouldn't budge. He kept his fists up before his face, watching Gabe, and waiting for a chance. Blood trailed from his nose and the corner of his mouth. Gabe's one good shot had done some good, but he knew it would take two or three like the first to bring Holzer to his knees, and Gabe wasn't sure he could manage that.

Suddenly, Holzer came at him, fists moving like pistons. Gabe stepped aside, but Holzer was ready for that. He lowered his head and slammed Gabe back, using his weight to keep Gabe off balance. Gabe landed one blow after another, but Holzer kept coming. He wrapped his big arms around Gabe, and Gabe felt his feet leave the ground.

Holzer lunged ahead and bulled Gabe off the landing dock and into the water. Gabe went under and felt his back sink into the mud. Holzer pommeled him with his fists. The water was scarcely six inches deep, but that was enough if you couldn't come up for air.

Gabe gasped for breath, brought up his damaged left, and pounded Holzer solidly in the eye. Holzer roared and leaped back, bringing one hand up to his face. Gabe went after him, dragging his boots through the mud. Grabbing Holzer's wet hair, he hauled back his right for a finishing blow.

"Just hold it, mister! Back off!"

Gabe froze, looked up, and saw a woman standing at the end of the dock, aiming a shotgun at his head. Gabe dropped Holzer and let him fall. Holzer sat down hard in the water and gasped for air.

The woman handed the shotgun to Keetch, put her hands on her hips, and grinned at Gabe.

"You done all right, mister," she said. "I haven't seen many could stand up to him 'long as that." She shook her head at Holzer. "Git up out of there and dry yourself for supper. By God, you look like a hog's been wallerin' in a sty!"

The men gathered around the woman laughed. Holzer stood and turned on Gabe.

"I ain't through with you, mister," he said. "Damned if I am."

"I'll count on it," Gabe said.

Holzer slogged out of the creek and stomped away. Keetch stretched out a hand and helped Gabe to dry land. The woman looked at Gabe, then past him. Elaine had been hidden by the crowd, but now she walked up beside Gabe. The woman studied Elaine a long moment, then her features softened to a smile.

"By God, you've grown up, but I bet I'd know you anywhere. Come and give your ma a hug, child, you ain't too old for that."

"Oh, mother!" Elaine looked stunned. Then she gave a joyous cry and ran into the woman's arms. Tears filled her eyes; the woman laughed, hugged her hard, then gripped her shoulders and held her off.

"Let my look at you, girl. They said you was a beauty, but you're some more'n that. Damned if you're not. Sure don't look like your father. Thank the good Lord you took after me."

"If I did, mother, I consider it a gift. You're the most beautiful lady I ever saw."

"Git on with you, child." The woman patted Elaine lightly on the bottom and smiled. "Guess I'll have to get used to this 'mother' business. Been a spell since anyone's called me anything but Lil."

Lil looked past her daughter and studied Gabe. "What kind of company you keeping, Elaine? You goin' to introduce us or what?"

"This is Gabe Conrad, mother," Elaine said. "Gabe came with me to help me find you."

"Hmmmph!" Lil scowled at Gabe. "Looks like you found yourself more than you bargained for, mister."

"Holzer and I have met a couple of times before," Gabe said. "We're sorta getting reacquainted again."

Gabe paused and looked Lil in the eyes. "I'm kind of surprised to find him here, ma'am, you don't mind me saying. There's some folks back in Jefferson who'd like to sit and talk with him a while."

Lil studied Gabe a long time and then smiled. "What folks in Jefferson, Texas want don't matter a lot to me. You might ought to think on that."

Lil glanced at Marshall and frowned. "Who's he? He belong to you?"

Elaine looked hurt and surprised. She opened her mouth to speak, but Lil quickly waved her off.

"My name's John Marshall," the black man said. "And I don't guess I belong to anyone but me, ma'am."

Lil spat and turned to Elaine. "Come on, let's you and me git somethin' to eat. We got a lot of talking to do."

Lil stopped and looked vaguely in Gabe's direction. "Guess you can come, too, if you like. Keetch'll git you some dry clothes."

Lil put her arm around Elaine and walked off through the trees. Gabe heard a muffled laugh behind him and saw Keetch leaning against a pole on the dock.

"Something funny, I don't guess I see it," said Gabe.

"No offense, mister," Keetch grinned. "You had this kinda look on your face is all. Everybody meets Lil, they usually get a look like that. Lil sorta gets your attention, so to speak."

"She does that, all right." Gabe picked up his pack.

Keetch looked at Marshall. "Go on over to the place 'bout three houses down thataway. Got a 'gator head over the door. The old man there'll get you somethin' to eat."

Marshall looked at Gabe. "I'd stick around close," Gabe said, warning Marshall with his eyes. "I'll get back soon as I can."

Marshall nodded and walked away. Gabe hadn't missed the fact that Keetch hadn't invited Marshall to *his* place. It was clear that a black man wasn't welcome here; Gabe didn't like the idea of leaving him on his own, but there was nothing he could do about that.

Gabe followed Keetch down a pathway through a heavy stand of pine. The houses were ramshackle dwellings, put together with whatever was available at the time. There were hovels of driftwood and dried palmetto fronds and a few with tin siding someone had brought in from outside.

A few women looked up from their chores as Gabe passed. They were all pale and lean-featured, cheerless women who betrayed no emotions at all. It was clear life was hard in the Thicket, and Gabe wondered, not for the first time, why anyone would choose such a place if they could possibly be anywhere else.

The children he saw playing in the dirt were big-bellied and spindle-legged, their small ribs visible under match stick arms. Gabe knew they looked this way because they seldom got the right things to eat. A diet of fried meat and lard took its toll. He'd heard people outside the Thicket call these folks clay eaters, because their children had skin yellow as tallow. Those who didn't die young of chills and fever grew up tough and mean. They didn't even know about anyplace else and thought the folks who lived outside the Thicket were peculiar, not them. Gabe decided that was why they didn't leave. Wherever you were, that's what seemed right to you. He had often heard whites say they didn't know how anyone could live like an Indian. And the Indians said the same thing about the whites. They couldn't understand how a man could wrap himself up in a hot suit and sleep in a cramped house. It wasn't civilized, Gabe had heard the Lakota say in their own way as he grew up. And when he entered the white world himself, he couldn't help but agree.

Keetch finally stopped before a weathered shack covered with pepper vines.

"Here we are," he said and invited Gabe in. "Ain't a lot, but it'll do."

Gabe saw that Keetch was right. The floor was dirt, and there were a few pieces of homemade furniture about. Keetch pawed through a pile of clothes and came up with a ragged shirt and a threadbare pair of trousers.

"Don't guess they'll fit, but reckon they'll do," Keetch said.

"I'm sure grateful," Gabe said politely, "but I wouldn't want

to put you out. I got some extra stuff in my pack."

Keetch stared as Gabe brought out a blue work shirt and a pair of denim pants.

"Lord help us," Keetch said, "you got *two* sets of good clothes? If that don't beat all."

"This here's about it," Gabe said. "Everything I own's in the pack."

"Uh-huh." It was clear Keetch didn't believe Gabe didn't own a wealth of extra garments. It looked like there was a hell of a lot of stuff in that pack. He muttered to himself and stepped out to let Gabe change.

Gabe stripped off his wet and muddy clothes, did his best to dry off, and was in his extra shirt and pants when Keetch returned.

While Keetch was gone, Gabe had time to take care of another matter that needed his attention. Keetch had taken his Colt at Holzer's command, but he'd left the shoulder holster alone, and he hadn't seen the knife that Gabe had sewn to the holster's back. Now, while Keetch was out of sight, he took the knife, ripped the sheath off the holster, and hid the knife and sheath behind his belt, leaving his shirt hanging loose. He left the shoulder holster in plain sight where Keetch could see it. Keetch had openly admired the shoulder rig, and Gabe wanted to make it easy for him to steal. Keetch was no prize, but he seemed a lot friendlier than the other Thicket dwellers Gabe had seen, and he had an idea he'd need all the help he could get in this place.

"You're ready, I'll take you over to Lil's place," Keetch said. "Boy, that's sure a nice shirt. What'd you have to give for it?"

Gabe said he couldn't recall. The hint was broad enough, and he decided he had another item to help him buy Keetch's friendship. By the time we're all through, Gabe thought grimly, I'll likely be walking around naked. Which is fine, if it'll get us out of here.

Lil's shack was set back amid thick palmetto palms and looked a hair neater than the rest. Keetch showed Gabe the way in and then left.

Lil and Elaine were sitting at a worn, wooden table, leaning

in close to each other, and talking up a storm. Gabe stood in shadow, just inside the door; the two were engrossed in one another and didn't seem to know he was there.

Seeing the women together again, Gabe was struck by how much they looked alike. Lil was nearly as tall as her daughter and had the same dark hair and striking green eyes. She had filled out a little more than Elaine, but all in the right places. There wasn't an ounce of fat on Lil where it shouldn't ought to be. From the story Elaine had told him about her mother, she was barely over forty; she didn't look a day older than thirty, and could easily be mistaken for Elaine's big sister.

Except for the eyes, Gabe thought. The color is the same, but the resemblance sure ends right there.

There was always a spark of mischief in Elaine's eyes, and Gabe knew very well the pleasure that special glow could bring. When he looked in Lil's eyes at the dock, he could find no warmth there at all. Lil could laugh easily with her mouth, but the laughter never touched her green eyes. Her eyes were flat and empty, cold, with no love in them at all.

Elaine couldn't see this, Gabe knew. What she saw was her mother, returned to her after lost years. And there's no way to tell her, Gabe thought. No way to show her that the mother she remembered died a long time ago, that the woman she'd found in the Thicket had eyes like a cottonmouth snake.

Gabe turned away and walked back into the dark. He could find his supper somewhere else. He didn't want to go in there with Lil. Lil would look right at him and know exactly what he saw in her eyes.

CHAPTER SEVENTEEN

Gabe had a bowl of stew with Keetch and tried not to think of what kind of meat was floating on the top. When the night closed in for good, he took his pack to a corner and went to sleep. There were roaches as big as mice everywhere, but he was too tired to think about that.

In the morning, Keetch was gone. Gabe's host hadn't left any breakfast around, so he dug a chunk of dried meat from his pack. The sun was still low in the east, but the settlement was already stifling hot. The odor of garbage, stale water, and decay hung on the air.

Gabe's first thought of the day was what the hell he was going to do next. Holzer was here, and Gabe was certain he was somehow connected to the events in Jefferson, Texas. And that meant Caddo Jack. Holzer and a half-breed killer. And Elaine's mother Lil. Where did she fit in? For Elaine's sake, he hoped she didn't fit in at all. Maybe she was just acquainted with Holzer, but didn't know anything about him. There was likely more than one undesirable character in the Thicket, resting up or on the run.

He saw Elaine coming, walking briskly down the path, ducking under somber gray strands of Spanish moss. Even in these dreary surroundings, among the makeshift homes, refuse, and

potbellied children, Elaine managed to look grand. The girl's got a talent for that, Gabe thought. Everything else seems to change, but Elaine is always the same.

"Gabe, I am *so* angry with you." Elaine came to him and kissed him soundly on the mouth. "Mother was expecting you for supper, and you never showed up."

"Figured you two had a lot of catching up to do," Gabe said. "Seemed like you ought to have some time alone."

"Oh, we had a marvelous time." Elaine grinned and shook her head in wonder. "My mother—honestly, you cannot imagine the things she's done, the places she's been. She's been about everywhere, Gabe. She even lived in Paris, France!"

"Now that's something."

"Gabe, I can't tell you how happy I am." Elaine wrapped her arms around his waist and rested her head on his shoulder. "Mother's been through so much. She's had some good times, but they don't make up for the bad."

Elaine stepped back and looked at Gabe. "I told her everything. What happened to Uncle Josh and William and Corette. She's heard about Caddo Jack, of course. Just about everyone around here has. She says he's likely in the Thicket, all right, but nobody knows where. She said to tell you it'd be a fool's errand to try and track him down. There's so many places to hide, Caddo Jack could be anywhere."

"Uh-huh." Gabe looked past Elaine and saw a patch of black water through the trees. "She say anything about Holzer, Elaine? What he's doing here?"

"No, she didn't, Gabe. Why should she?"

Gabe wasn't looking at her then, but he could hear the sudden chill in her voice.

"Just wondering, is all," he said casually. "You can see how I might be concerned. The man's tried to gun me down once. He'd be happy as a clam if I was dead, and we're both right here in a pretty small place."

"Of course I can see why you're concerned. But that has nothing to do with my mother. Gabe, will you please look at me?"

Gabe faced her and gripped her shoulders. "I never said he had anything to do with your mother. All right? I didn't say

that. I'm just curious why he's here. I told you once, Elaine. You can't just wish trouble away. It'll follow you around, even if you run off to the Thicket. The way I see it, that's what we've got here. Holzer's mixed up in that mess back in Jefferson. I'm dead certain of that. I don't know how, but he is."

Elaine waved his words aside. "You don't like Holzer, and I sure can't blame you for that. But I think your feelings for the man have colored your thinking somewhat."

"All right."

"All right what?"

"All right, Elaine, we won't talk about it anymore."

"Good. I don't think we should." Elaine brushed back her hair. "As a matter of fact, mother said she'd talk to this Holzer. She said that whatever happened between you two on the outside, you'd best *keep* it outside and not here."

"And you think Holzer will go along with that?"

"I think he'd *better*." Elaine raised a brow. "Mother has a lot of friends here. People listen to what she says; I know that."

"Fine with me, then." Gabe didn't remind her that Holzer seemed to have a lot of clout here, too. Enough to take Gabe's Colt, and stay armed himself. That fact didn't add much weight to Lil's assurance.

"Oh, and mother wants you to come to dinner," Elaine said. "At noon. She said she hasn't had much of a chance to get to know you, and she won't be stood up again."

"I'll be there, then," Gabe said.

"Oh, Gabe." Elaine wrapped her arms around his neck and drew him close. "You'll like her when you get to know her. Honestly you will."

"I don't have any reason not to like her right now," Gabe said, hoping the lie didn't show. "She's your mother, and that's enough for me."

"Noon then, all right?" She looked into his eyes. "I miss you, Gabe. I miss having you hold me, and—and doing all the things you do."

Elaine pressed the length of her body against him. Gabe felt his mouth go dry. The touch of her brought back every moment of the nights they'd had together.

"I miss you, too," he said. "I'm hoping we can find us some time alone soon."

"Oh, we will, Gabe." She gave him a mischievous wink, turned, and walked back the way she'd come.

Gabe watched her go. He stood in the hot morning and looked after her long after she disappeared in the trees.

She's blind to everything, he thought. She can't see what's in her mother's eyes, and she's not about to try. All she knows is what she's been holding in her heart all these years. And that isn't anywhere close to what's real.

Gabe walked north past Keetch's house on a path that led through the trees. There were very few shacks in this direction. The land narrowed down to next to nothing past the settlement itself. He followed a sluggish creek to his left and found it deepened to relatively clear water. Following the hard-packed dirt path, he passed a marshy inlet where weathered planks and old bricks were laid out to cover the mud. Dugout canoes, and larger, flat-bottomed pirogues were beached here. A graybearded man with a shotgun sat on the dock and gave Gabe a wary look.

Gabe smiled at the old man and got nothing in return. They guarded the boats, then. Only one man—or only one that Gabe could see. He had an idea there were people everywhere, that he was never entirely alone in this place. He was free to go anywhere he liked, or so it seemed. That was an illusion, he knew. If he tried to go where they didn't want him to go— in one of those boats, for instance—a bearded figure with a gun would pop up from behind a log.

Farther upstream, Gabe found the shore lined with sycamore and cherrybark oak. A frayed rope hung over a natural swimming hole. He tried to imagine the jaundiced, unhealthy looking children he'd seen laughing and playing here, but couldn't bring the image to mind. Standing still, he could hear the shriek of birds off in the swamp. And from somewhere far away, the deep grunt of a big bull gator.

Gabe figured it was getting close to noon, and it seemed like a good idea to be on time for dinner. Lil was a woman who liked to have her way. Gabe could see now that Elaine

Snaketown

had picked up this quality from her mother and father both. Robert Porter and Lil weren't anything alike, but they were both about as stubborn as a Tennessee mule.

Two minutes after he'd started back, Gabe paused to get his bearings. He was headed toward the settlement, but he discovered he had strayed off the path. The creek had disappeared, and the pathway here was overgrown with vines and weeds. For a moment, he considered going back, then decided it would take too much time. The route wasn't easy, but he could hear people talking in the distance and knew the settlement couldn't be far away.

Gabe walked a few yards and then stopped. There was a hole in the ground on the way ahead. The hole was nearly perfectly round and five feet or so across. Gabe moved up carefully and looked down.

A chill touched the back of his neck. The pit was ten feet deep and full of snakes. Gabe could smell the peculiar, dry-sweet odor of the creatures. The snakes writhed and hissed, roiling about in a mass like the entrails of some monster in a child's nightmare. There were copperheads and canebrake rattlers and cottonmouth moccasins with bellies white as death. There were hundreds of them in the pit, some as big around as Gabe's thighs.

What the hell was this doing here? he wondered. Someone had a strange idea of pets. There was nothing you could do with a snake except kill it or leave it alone. They weren't good for anything else.

For an instant, the real world seemed to slide away. Gabe could see a Lakota shaman around his fire, spinning tales of the spirits that lived in this world and the next. Gabe was Long Rider, the boy, and the pit full of snakes was there, too. The shaman was slick with the heat of his fire. He carried a bone-white knife in one hand and a gourd rattle in the other. He stuck the knife in his mouth, and it turned into a set of serpent fangs. He tapped the gourd against his foot, and the foot became a tail. The tail rattled, and the snake mouth hissed. A forked tongue flicked out of the shaman's mouth. The shaman tried to talk to Long Rider, but the boy couldn't make out his words. All he could hear was a rattle and a hiss.

The shaman was trying to warn the boy, Gabe knew. The same way a river spirit had tried to tell Gabe what would happen to Lucas Harrow. Something would happen again, couldn't the foolish boy see that? Had he forgotten the Lakota ways?

Gabe felt himself falling. He opened his eyes and saw he was swaying close to the edge of the pit. With a short cry of alarm, he caught himself and backed away.

"Lord God, mister, what the hell you tryin' to do?"

"What? Who's that?" Gabe turned, startled to see Keetch standing behind him.

"If I was you, I wouldn't hang around this place," Keetch said. He looked warily over his shoulder and back to Gabe. "This ain't a real good place to be."

"No, no I guess not." Gabe could smell his own sweat. He didn't look at the pit again.

"Best you be gettin' back," Keetch said. "I'll show you the way."

Gabe followed Keetch back to the settlement. The day seemed the same as before, muggy and green. Except for the spirit dream. The fear left him almost at once, but the spirit dream refused to go away.

"Most of your damn outsiders don't know a blessed thing about the Thicket," Lil said. "Think we're nothing but a bunch of ignorant crackers in here." Lil winked at Gabe. "I 'spect that thought's crossed your mind more'n once, Mr. Gabe Conrad. Don't say it hasn't. I'm a swamp woman, but I'm not real dumb."

"Never thought anything of the kind," Gabe said, clearing his throat. "My way of thinking, folks are about the same everywhere."

"Ha!" Lil poked a fork in the air. "You're a liar, mister, but you sure are a good-lookin' liar, I got to say that." She turned and poked playfully at Elaine. "I've always had a way with the menfolk, child. I reckon I passed it along to you."

"Mother!" Elaine colored and glanced quickly at Gabe.

"Well, no use denyin' fact. No use at all."

Snaketown

Lil raised a tin cup, drained it, and smacked her lips. "Truth's truth, I always say, and isn't any way you're ever goin' to get around it."

Gabe hoped that Lil's dinner would end soon, but there was no sign that it was coming to a halt. Lil liked to eat, drink, and hear herself talk. There was plenty to drink, a table full of food, and, Gabe suspected, the woman seldom ran out of something to say.

Lil's house was comfortable enough, a hundred percent better than Keetch's place. There were straw mattress beds, keg chairs, and a stone fireplace. Quilts adorned the walls, bright patchwork covers colored with indigo and red oak dyes. The floor was hard-packed dirt, but it was clean.

Gabe had enjoyed the meal. There were pumpkin yams, boiled hominy grits, cucumbers, and turnip greens. The meat was pork, wood hog likely butchered and smoked the year before, and heavy with salt. There was bread for a fork and lard for a spread. Gabe recalled the potbellied children he had seen and wondered if everyone in the settlement ate as well as Lil. It didn't seem likely that they did.

It wasn't the setting or the food that bothered Gabe. It was Lil and the homemade whiskey she poured from an ivory-colored crock. There were all kinds of drinkers in the world, Gabe knew. Happy drinkers and drinkers who liked to cry. Drinkers who simply passed out and went to sleep. Lil was a mean drinker; Gabe was sure of that. Dinner wasn't half over before Lil was into her crock.

Even Elaine, who refused to see her mother's faults, was showing some concern. She was smiling so much, Gabe was sure her mouth would crack.

"Truth," said Lil, "now that's somethin' your father didn't know nothin' about. Tell you that right now . . . didn't know the firs' thing 'bout the truth."

"This is sure fine pork," Gabe put in. "Guess you grow the hogs right here. I'd like to see 'em sometime."

Lil showed him a glazed and puzzled look, as if Gabe might be speaking Chinese.

"Your father, now thas a real lyin' sumbitch. You know that?"

"Father does his best I think, mother," Elaine said evenly. "I know he's made a lot of mistakes. I mean, all the trouble between you two . . ." Elaine's voice trailed off.

"Mistakes?" Lil frowned and licked her fingers. "Is that what you call it? God, honey, you don't know the bastard, and thas' the truth."

Lil tried to find her crock and knocked over a bowl of syrup. Elaine quickly set it right.

"Grow these turnips here, too?" Gabe asked. "Say, I didn't know you could do that much with vegetables out here."

"Want to hear about truth and men who tell you lies?" Lil's head swayed as she leaned in close to Elaine. "Robert tol' you 'bout how old Josh raped that Indian girl when he was young? I bet he told you that."

"Yes he did, mother. But that was a long time ago."

"Wasn't too damn long," Lil said. She blinked and gave Elaine a silly grin. "Wasn't Josh Porter done it, either."

"What?" Elaine's face went slack. "What are you—talking about, mother? Of course it was Josh. Who else would it—"

"Lil," Gabe began.

"Wasn't him at all," Lil said. "It was Robert who did it, child. Your ol' daddy, the one who makes—mistakes. Tol' me all about it one night. Man always tol' me ever'thing. Hell, what I had to give him, he'd tell me anything was on his mind. Raped that girl and told Josh that *he* did it. Damn fool Josh was too drunk to know better. Robert raped the girl and shot her father dead. Dragged Josh back to their camp. And—and when the whiskey wore off, he tol' Josh it was him who'd done the rapin' and the killin' himself."

Lil threw back her head and laughed. "Bastard got even for the way Josh treated him, that's for sure. Tol' Josh what he'd done and left him there for good. Never seen him again and never tol' him it wasn't him. Got even, all right."

"Oh my God!" Elaine's eyes filled with tears, and her features contorted in pain. "That's not true, mother. You're just—saying that because you hate him so much! He couldn't *do* a thing like that!"

"Lil, you haven't any right to tell your daughter such things," Gabe said angrily. "I don't know if it's a lie or not. But you

don't have any cause to try and hurt her like this."

Lil's eyes were half closed. She tried to grin, but the muscles wouldn't work the way they should.

"Wants his big secret kept," Lil said. "Don't want any of his high-livin' friends to know what he is. But *I* know, I'll tell you that. Know lots of things . . ."

Lil stared at Gabe, and for an instant she was sober as a judge. "I know he's coming. Don't think I don't. Knows I'm in here, too. Knows I'm right here. Took me out of the swamp and dressed me up real nice. But I came back. Left him and came back here where I belong. Woman can't—live with a man like that. Damn—liar is what he is."

"Oh, mother. Oh God, mother!" Elaine clutched a hand to her breast.

Lil suddenly went limp and dropped her head on one arm. She started snoring, and her mouth went slack.

Gabe stood quickly and went to Elaine. "Come on, let's go," he said.

Elaine shook him off. "I can't. I've got to stay with her."

"Like hell you do," Gabe said. He lifted her up, grasped her shoulders, and led her out into the afternoon sun. Elaine cried and protested, but Gabe had no intention of letting her go.

CHAPTER EIGHTEEN

"You don't want to get yourself all worked up," Gabe said. "Your mother was drinking, Elaine. You don't know if any of that stuff was true or not. Drinkin's got a way of twisting folks' heads around wrong."

"It sounded so real, Gabe," Elaine said. "Only I know it couldn't have happened that way. Father wouldn't do a thing like that. He couldn't!"

The day was hot as a furnace. Gabe could feel Elaine tremble in his arms. They stood beneath a giant cypress, close to the water, near the landing wharf where they had first come upon the settlement. Nearly everyone had gone inside to sleep away the heat, and they had the place all to themselves.

"I don't think he could either," Gabe said. He wasn't sure he thought that at all, but it wouldn't help any to share his doubts with Elaine. "What I think is, your mother's had a lot of years to work up a real anger for your father. And anger's got a way of feeding on itself. If you don't do anything about it, it keeps on getting bigger all the time."

"And you think that's what mother's done?"

"I think it's real likely, I sure do. Lil's feelings for your father are pretty twisted up. She isn't going to see any good in

the man; she's going to see the worst. By now, she probably believes that's the way things happened back then between your father and your Uncle Josh. 'Cause that's what she wants to believe."

"You think so?" Elaine looked hopefully at Gabe, and Gabe wiped a tear from her eye.

"Yes I do, Elaine." He led her away from the dock, back down the shaded path. "What I want you to do, is leave your mother alone for a while. Let her sleep it off. Talk to her later on this evening some time. You can rest up at Keetch's. He won't bother you any; Keetch is all right."

"And what are you going to do? You're not going to leave me there, are you?"

"Just for a while," Gabe assured her. "I won't be gone long. I want to look around some."

A shadow of concern crossed Elaine's features. "I don't want you to get in any trouble, Gabe. Promise me you won't do that."

Gabe forced a smile. "Now what kind of trouble would I likely get into, Elaine?"

"Holzer, for a start," she said solemnly. "Stay away from him, Gabe."

"I'll do that," Gabe said. He stopped in front of Keetch's shack. "Hell, I'm still sore from last time. I'm sure not looking for a fight."

Gabe walked back past the dock, skirting the path to Lil's house. He hoped what he'd told Elaine was true, that her mother was sleeping off a drunk. If she wasn't, he didn't want to chance running into her again.

Locusts sawed away in the trees as he made his way toward the far end of the island. He knew all about the other end; there was nothing there to see except dark water and a pit full of snakes. Gabe didn't care if he never saw that sight again.

Past the last shack in the settlement, the island seemed to stretch out wide. This part of the land had been cleared long ago of trees and brush. There were small garden plots and even a field of stunted corn. Beyond the field was another thicket of trees and wooden pens of rough-cut timber. Gabe could smell

the presence of hogs before he even got close. The odor was likely bad enough any time of the year, but was something close to awful in the stifling summer heat.

A bearded man in filthy coveralls lay in a hammock in front of his shack. A hat covered his eyes. As Gabe passed by, the man raised the hat with his brow, took a good look, then went back to sleep. Gabe could hear a child bawling in the shack. He walked on toward the pens, turned a corner of the fence, and spotted John Marshall. Marshall was hauling buckets of slop from a big pot and tossing them into the pens.

"I see you got a job," Gabe said. "Nice to see a man learning a trade."

Marshall set down his buckets and wiped his hands along his pants. "Fella sleepin' over there told me this here's slave's work," he grumbled. "Wanted to ask him who done it 'fore I come along."

"Probably a good thing you didn't."

"Same thing occurred to me. 'Specially since I know it was him. Miss Elaine, she doin' all right?"

"She could be better," Gabe said. He quickly told Marshall what had happened at Lil's, and what the woman had said about Robert Porter and his brother. When he finished, Marshall frowned thoughtfully and looked at the ground.

"I've worked for Mr. Robert seven years. Meanin' no disrespect, but anything you told me 'bout the man, I'd say there's a chance you was right. He's got a meanness in his soul. Somethin' way down deep."

"So you think what Lil said might be true."

"Don't want to think anyone'd do a thing like that."

"But Porter's capable of something like that?"

"That business 'tween him and Mr. Josh was a long time ago. But I don't figure folks change a whole lot. Leastways for the better they don't."

Gabe leaned over the fence and looked down into the pens. Big razorback hogs snorted and rolled in the mud under great clouds of swollen blue flies. One old boar gazed at Gabe with tiny eyes. Gabe guessed the creature had to weigh something over three hundred pounds. Ugly yellow tusks curled up from

Snaketown

the bottom of its jaw, met strong upper teeth, and clicked out a challenge to Gabe.

"They ain't real pretty," Marshall said, guessing Gabe's thoughts. "Not real friendly critters, either. Wouldn't get me in that pen on a bet."

Gabe glanced over his shoulder at the man in the hammock. "We've got to get out of here, John. I don't know just how, but we'd better figure a way. I've got some bad feelings about this place. Elaine thinks everything'll be just fine because of her mother, but I'm not counting on that."

Marshall nodded slowly, took off his straw hat, and wiped sweat from his face. "There's something else, too. Maybe you know it, but I figure you haven't had the chance to find out." He glanced off west through the trees. "There's more folks hangin' 'round this place than you think. People that stay out there and don't never come in."

Gabe frowned. "What do you mean? People out where?"

"Out there, across the swamp. This island drops off maybe fifty yards down from the pens. There's swamp after that for another hundred yards, then there's some kinda land past that. You can't see a lot, but you can hear 'em and see their fires at night. Real early this morning, I walked out a ways to do my business, and I seen a bunch of boats, them long pirogues, like the one that Keetch brung us on. Ten, maybe a dozen boats, all of 'em full of men, and every one of them carrying guns. They pulled up quiet like and joined the men that was already there."

Gabe let out a breath. "What do you think they're doing, John? If they're that close to this island, they're a part of this settlement, too. Everybody here knows they're there."

"Sure as hell do," Marshall said. "These swampers know where every snake and bug is hidin' out within twenty miles of this place."

"They belong here, then, but they're keeping out of sight," Gabe finished. He thought about the McCabe clan and all the other settlements that must be hidden about the Thicket. "You can bet they aren't hiding from us. They're over there in case some of the neighbors drop by."

Marshall gave Gabe a sober look. "What are they doing, though? They sure ain't campin' out for fun."

"If you see a band of armed men in one spot, they're getting ready to do something to somebody else. That's a war party over there, John. You and me just don't know where the war is." Gabe frowned. "Holzer. That's what he's here for. You can bet on that."

Gabe grasped Marshall by the shoulders. "Whatever you do, *don't* go wandering off in that direction again. It isn't going to be real easy to get the three of us out of this place. We won't have any chance at all if they think we know about that army over there."

"I don't talk to no one but these hogs," Marshall said. He forced a smile and looked at Gabe. "You and me and Miss Elaine's going to get out of here. Don't much care for the pig trade, I'll tell you that."

"We'll get out. Count on it, John." Gabe took a step to the right so the man in the hammock couldn't possibly see John Marshall. He drew the sheathed blade from under his shirt and slipped it in Marshall's hands.

"Here, you keep this," he said. "They're likely to find it quicker on me than on you."

"That don't leave you with nothing," Marshall said.

"If I can't get a hold of more than that," Gabe said, "it isn't going to matter a lot."

Gabe left Marshall and walked back toward the settlement. Talk's one thing, he thought bitterly, and doing's something else. Getting in this place is a hell of a lot easier than getting out.

He thought about Robert Porter's posse, riding around somewhere in the Thicket. He figured Keetch was right. You could send a thousand men in here, and it wouldn't do a damn bit of good if they all got lost in the swamp. There was no use looking for help from outside. If he and John Marshall and Elaine got out of the swamp in one piece, they'd have to do it by themselves.

And that means killing Holzer, Gabe thought grimly. Holzer and maybe half the male population of the settlement. It didn't seem like a real good plan. Sneaking off somehow without telling anyone good-bye was a better idea. All he had to figure out was how.

CHAPTER NINETEEN

Gabe heard the crowd shouting, then saw them through the trees. They were gathered in front of Lil's house. Gabe figured there were maybe two hundred people in the settlement; men, women, and children; and they all seemed to be on hand.

He spotted Keetch and Elaine at the edge of the crowd and quickly went to them. Elaine looked relieved and held on tightly to his arm.

"What the hell's going on?" Gabe asked. "It isn't Christmas yet, I know that."

"Goin' to have us a celebration," Keetch grinned. "Real big'un, I'd say."

"What for?"

Keetch answered, but Gabe couldn't hear his words. At that moment, the crowd looked back to the north, tossed their straw hats in the air, and opened up their ranks.

A tall, solidly built man broke through into the open. He was naked to the waist, and thick cords of muscle sheathed his shoulders and arms. His powerful legs were encased in dirty buckskin pants, and his feet were bare. A red band circled his brow, and raven-black hair hung down his back. Dark skin was stretched tightly over his features, and his eyes were black as

tar. He stood in the middle of the cheering crowd, waving a brand new Winchester rifle above his head.

Elaine felt Gabe stiffen at her side. She looked up curiously and caught her breath, shaken by the expression on his face.

"Gabe?"

Gabe didn't answer. He pushed Elaine behind him and stared at the man in the clearing. He'd only seen the man for fleeting seconds, but he would never forget that face. The instant Caddo Jack pulled the trigger and blew Lucas Harrow apart, his features were branded forever in Gabe's mind. The cold, black eyes. The sheer look of pleasure on the man's face.

The half-breed seemed to sense Gabe's attention. He turned slowly from the crowd and looked directly at Gabe. His eyes went wide, and a broad grin split his features. He raised one hand from his side and pointed it like a weapon.

"I know you," he said. "This time I killin' you good." His voice was like gravel in a can. "I think I doin' this now."

Caddo Jack tossed his rifle aside and whipped a long knife from his belt. Gabe reached for the blade beneath his shirt, then suddenly remembered he'd given it to John. He glanced around quickly, spotted a pile of wood by Lil's door, and snatched up a fair-sized piece of kindling.

Caddo Jack pointed at Gabe's weapon and laughed. Elaine cried out in fear and started for Gabe. Keetch reached out and pulled her aside.

The half-breed glanced at Elaine and grinned. "Pretty," he said. "Real pretty woman, I think." His smile faded at once, and he came at Gabe in a crouch, the blade pressed tightly against his leg.

Gabe hefted the club in his hand and watched the man move. He held the knife the way he should, loose and low, his motions fluid as a snake's. Gabe knew his weapon was no match for the knife. The only way he'd come out whole was to strike the first blow, and Caddo Jack wouldn't let him do that. He'd patiently circle Gabe, wait for his moment, and plunge the blade home.

The half-breed moved in a blur. Gabe jerked back and felt steel whip past his cheek. He swung his club and missed. Caddo Jack grinned, shifted on his feet, and came in low, his

body bent nearly to the ground. He stalked Gabe from the left, then weaved to the right, moving in and moving out.

Gabe stood his ground. He knew what the half-breed was doing. He was deliberately inviting Gabe to strike, leaving himself open, trying to draw his opponent in. Fine, Gabe thought grimly, that business works two ways, friend.

The next time Caddo Jack shifted to the left, Gabe feinted in that direction, bent low, and then threw himself to the right, bringing up his weapon from the knees. The half-breed wasn't taken in. He moved faster than Gabe had ever imagined a man could move. Gabe's blow missed by a mile, and Caddo Jack's knife flashed out, slashing across Gabe's chest and drawing blood, driving Gabe back with one vicious slash after another. Gabe ducked under Caddo Jack's powerful arm, came up, and hit the man a glancing blow on his shoulder. The half-breed kept coming; he shifted the blade smoothly from his left hand to his right, daring Gabe to try again.

Gabe feinted with his club, and Caddo Jack jumped away. Gabe kicked out with his boot and struck the man solidly in the belly. Caddo Jack looked surprised. He grinned at Gabe and came in again. Gabe backed off. Caddo Jack lashed out, faking a thrust to Gabe's chest, then bringing the knife up hard. The blade caught Gabe's stick of wood and jerked it out of his hand. Caddo Jack laughed.

Gabe heard Elaine cry out, and then the half-breed was on him, slashing at his arms, driving in to cut his face.

"All right, by God, let's quit this shit right now!"

Caddo Jack stopped in his tracks. Gabe glanced to his left and saw Lil. She stood in the doorway of her shack, Holzer at her side. Holzer was naked to the waist, and Lil was clearly half drunk. Her hair hung loosely about her face. Her blouse draped off of one shoulder, all but exposing her breast.

Gabe heard a muffled sound from Elaine, but kept his eyes on Caddo Jack.

The half-breed looked at Lil and frowned. "I'm goin' to stick him," he said shortly. "Got a right to do that. Want the pretty girl."

"Now, I don't think you ought to do that, Jack," Lil said calmly.

"I do what I want!" Caddo Jack screwed up his mouth and spat on the ground.

"No you don't, Jack. You listen to me. This ain't the right thing to do."

"Right's what *I* want to do!"

Lil let out a breath. "Jack, you go on about your business, now. You and me'll talk later on."

"Isn't nothing to talk about." Caddo Jack stood his ground, dark eyes flicking restlessly from Gabe to Elaine and back to Lil. "I'm goin' to stick him. Goin' to take me that girl."

Lil stepped boldly up to the half-breed and looked him in the eyes. "You ain't killin' anyone right now," she said sharply. "And you ain't takin' the girl. This youngun's mine; I told you that before."

"Don't matter none to me." Caddo Jack gave Lil a chilling look. "Goin' to do what I want."

Lil stood up straight. Confronting the half-breed had sobered her fast, Gabe saw. He could read the touch of fear in her eyes. She was scared to death of Caddo Jack. If she couldn't control him now, if he didn't back down, he might turn on her as well.

"Jack, git back to your place and stay there till I call you," Lil said, bringing all the strength she could muster to her voice. "You do what I'm saying, and you do it now. You understand me, boy?"

Gabe held his breath. The half-breed's eyes went flat as death. For an instant, Gabe was sure the man would strike down Lil on the spot. Then, Caddo Jack scowled and looked down at his feet. He looked at Lil once more, then turned and stomped off through the crowd.

Lil muttered something to herself and let her breath whistle through her teeth. She turned angrily on the crowd.

"Go on, git out of here," she said harshly, "there's nothing here to see!"

The people began to wander off. Gabe looked at Holzer. Holzer's face was pale as dough.

Lil turned to Elaine. "Git inside," she said bluntly. "Holzer, git this feller back to Keetch's place. Make sure he stays there, too."

"No!" Elaine held onto Gabe. "I want him here with me, mother."

"This don't concern him at all," Lil said.

"It sure as hell does!" Elaine blurted. Her eyes blazed with anger. "It concerns him and me, too. You've got a lot of explaining to do, mother. You *lied* to me. You said you didn't know that—that person, and it's very clear you know him quite well. I want some answers right now!"

"Isn't none of your business who I know and who I don't," Lil said shortly. "Now git on in the house, girl, 'less you want me to throw you in."

"Be real pleased to help." Holzer grinned. "Wouldn't be no trouble at all."

Elaine's face went dark with rage. "If you're going to—to consort with that man, kindly don't do it in front of me!"

"Consort, is it?" Lil shook her head. "My, ain't we educated, now?"

"I don't see that's anything to be ashamed of," Elaine said. "As a matter of fact—"

"Elaine, why don't you give it up?" Gabe shook his head. "There isn't any use in talking, and there sure isn't anything here needs explaining. That trained maniac of your mother's killed your cousin and her husband, just like he killed your uncle Josh. It was her sent that letter to get him up here. She hates your father so much she'd do damn near anything."

Gabe turned on Lil. "I'd say you 'bout pushed that killer of yours about as far as you can go. You've got a stick of dynamite out there, lady. He'll do what you say most of the time, but you aren't sure just when he'll go off. I was watching. You nearly lost him 'bout twice. Hell, he came that close to knifing you and carrying off your own daughter!"

Gabe looked at Holzer and grinned. "I know *you* saw it. You were right close to filling your pants. And I got news for you, mister. That fellow would've had your head in a sack before you squeezed off a shot. He isn't real slow, I'll tell you that."

"You close your mouth or I'll do it for you," Holzer raged.

"Shut up, both of you!" Lil snapped. She gave Gabe a killing look. "You through gabbing, mister? Well I sure as hell am.

Damn it, Holzer, I told you to get this bastard out of here. Take him back to Keetch's and get that other one, too. I don't want them two runnin' loose."

Elaine's eyes went wide. "What are you going to do to them, mother? You leave them alone!"

"Ain't goin' to do a thing 'cept keep 'em shut up."

"No, I won't have that. You can't!"

Holzer drew his pistol and rammed it hard in Gabe's chest. "You got about a minute to start walking," he said cheerfully. "I'd just as soon blow a hole in you right here."

"Can't resist an offer like that," Gabe said. He turned and started off across the clearing. Elaine called out, but he didn't look back. He didn't want to face her now. He knew for certain Lil had no intention of letting him and Marshall leave the settlement alive. Her eyes told him that. He was sure if he looked at Elaine, she could see the truth there, too.

"I'm real sorry 'bout this," Keetch said. "You never done me any harm, but I got to do what Miz Lil says."

"Not your fault," Gabe told him. "I don't blame you any, Keetch."

"Holzer don't want me to give you no water or anything, but I will. He sure don't like you very much."

"I don't like him a lot either, Keetch."

Keetch grinned. "You sure are takin' this good, I'll say that."

"I haven't got a whole lot of choice," Gabe said. He was lying on the floor of Keetch's hut, where Holzer had left him. The man had trussed him up good, bending his calves up tight against his thighs, then stretching his arms down to his ankles. It was all Gabe could do to simply breathe. He could move his head an inch to the right or to the left, but nothing more than that.

Keetch sat in a broken chair, tilted back against the open door, bare feet pressed against the frame. He held an ancient rifle in his lap. Gabe couldn't tell the make; the barrel was caked with rust, and the stock had been broken and bound back together with baling wire. Most likely, Gabe decided, the weapon would blow up and kill Keetch if he ever tried

Snaketown 139

to fire it. Not that it mattered, since Gabe was in no position to leap up and try to take the gun away.

He thought about John. It had been close to an hour since Holzer had brought Gabe to Keetch's and tied him up. If they were going to bring John here, too, it shouldn't take this long. Gabe had a bad feeling in his gut. Maybe they decided not to bother with John and simply shot him on the spot. Gabe didn't want to think about that.

"I was wondering," Gabe said, "you ever been out of this place, Keetch? I mean, to a town or anywhere."

Keetch screwed up his face in thought. "Been over to Votaw twice. Almost got to Liberty once, but something come up."

"What's Votaw like?"

"Little ol' squatty town. Don't amount to much."

"You like to go somewhere else, sometime? Houston, maybe over west to Fort Worth?"

Keetch's face brightened. "Lord, I sure would. Fort Worth, now that'd be somethin' to see."

"It's some kind of town, all right. I expect you'd like it a lot. Get yourself some fine clothes, a nice hat, and some boots. Meet a whole lot of pretty girls. Buy yourself a steak dinner and cold beer every night. Stay in a fine hotel."

Keetch's eyes went wide, then his brows came together in a frown. "What the hell you talkin' about, mister? I ain't ever goin' to do nothin' like that. Shit. That'd take all the money in the world."

"It'd take some, all right," Gabe said. "Hundred, two hundred dollars, a man could sure have him a month's worth of fun in Fort Worth."

"Two hundred dollars?" Keetch spat on the floor in disgust. "I ain't ever even seen that much."

Gabe took a deep breath. "I could give you the money, Keetch."

Keetch blinked. "What are you saying?"

" 'Course I sure can't give it to you here. I'm not carrying that kind of money around. If you were to—decide you'd like to see the sights, though, we could have ourselves a time."

"You're talkin' 'bout me letting you go, now ain't you?" Keetch put his feet on the floor and stared at Gabe. "Shoot.

You think I want to get my throat cut, mister?"

"Don't see any reason why we'd have to tell anyone we were leaving, Keetch. Listen, there's a couple of gals in Fort Worth, one of 'em I recall has got curly red hair—"

"I don't want to hear 'bout no gal with red hair," Keetch said gruffly.

"Suit yourself," Gabe said.

Keetch muttered something under his breath and leaned back in his chair. Gabe tried to move his hands and his feet. He couldn't feel anything at all. Another couple of hours and he'd lose both hands and his feet. Maybe that's what Holzer has in mind, he thought darkly. Let his limbs turn black, and then toss him in the swamp.

"What's she look like?" Keetch said suddenly.

"What's who look like?"

"Uh, that gal. You know, the one with red hair."

"*That* gal." Gabe winked at Keetch. "Never saw a woman like that before. Skin the color of milk. Legs that'll wrap around you twice."

Keetch stared at Gabe. "You—you done that with her?"

"Sure have. You could, too. 'Course, you got to go to Fort Worth. She isn't coming here. And it's clear you don't want to go there."

"Didn't say I didn't *want* to go, now," Keetch protested.

"You don't care for redheads, there's this yellow-haired gal. She's got a pair of—"

Gabe stopped as a shadow crossed the door against the light. A bearded young man leaned down and spoke to Keetch. Keetch frowned, and the man went away.

"What's that all about?" Gabe asked.

Keetch scowled at him. "Nothing. I ain't supposed to say."

"All right."

Keetch made a noise in his throat. "Don't see how it'd do any harm. That pal of yours stole a boat and got away. Shit, I ain't real surprised."

Keetch grinned broadly. "Ol' Holzer was mad as a hornet. Went after him himself. Took a couple of good shooters with him, too. Lord God, I wouldn't be in your shoes, mister, if he don't bring that nigger back."

"Don't blame you," Gabe said. He said a silent prayer to whatever Lakota spirits might be listening at the moment. Maybe John would make it, but Gabe didn't give him half a chance. John was a smart, resourceful man, but it would take more than that to outfox some old Thicket hands in their own backyard. If they got him, Gabe hoped they wouldn't get him alive.

CHAPTER TWENTY

"That stuff about Fort Worth gals and all," Keetch said, "you can just quit talkin' bout that 'cause there's nothin' I can do. I can't let you loose, mister. Maybe I'd like to, but I can't. Sure can't after that pal of yours took off. Shit, that Holzer'd have my hide."

"He would if he caught you," Gabe said. "I figure you know the Thicket as well as he does, Keetch. I've seen you out there, remember, and I doubt there's a man could do better."

Keetch seemed pleased at that. "I reckon I know my way around."

"Hell yes, you do. Those McCabes never even saw you coming. And that was in broad daylight. There isn't anyone here who could catch you at night."

"Yeah, there is, too." Keetch stared at the wall of his shack and saw something there that made him shudder. He hunched his shoulders together and folded his arms tightly across his chest, as if he were trying to pull himself inside a shell.

"You're thinking of Caddo Jack," Gabe said.

Keetch didn't answer, but his eyes told Gabe all he needed to know.

"You want to tell me about him? What's he doing here,

Snaketown   143

Keetch? He doesn't belong here, I know that. What's he—"

"I don't know nothin' 'bout Caddo Jack," Keetch said angrily. "You just shut up about him, you hear?"

"All right, Keetch."

"Isn't anything to tell. Isn't nothin' you need to know."

Keetch squirmed around in his chair, muttering to himself. He looked to Gabe like a man who was sitting on a boil. That half-breed's got everyone in this settlement scared out of their wits, Gabe thought, everyone from Lil on down. Yet they gather around and cheer him when he appears, like he was some kind of hero come home. What the hell did he give them that was worth keeping a madman in their midst?

Gabe figured he'd been tied up on Keetch's floor maybe two or three hours. He'd asked Keetch twice to loosen his bonds, but Keetch refused to help. He had been friendly and talkative enough until Gabe mentioned Caddo Jack. After that, he had little at all to say.

Gabe could hear laughter and fiddle music and decided it was the big celebration in the clearing Keetch had mentioned. He asked Keetch what they were celebrating, but Keetch wouldn't reply. It clearly had something to do with Caddo Jack, Gabe knew. The half-breed had returned from somewhere and evidently brought good news. Gabe couldn't imagine what it was, but he was sure it wasn't anything he'd care to cheer about himself.

When the late afternoon turned to evening, Keetch, for some reason, had a change of heart, and fed Gabe a few bites of bread and pork and let him drink a cup of water. He still wouldn't touch the ropes, though he could see what the bonds were doing to Gabe's limbs. It was obvious he was frightened of Holzer, or Lil, or Caddo Jack, or possibly all three, and Gabe, in spite of his concern for gangrene, couldn't much blame him.

He worried about Elaine. Lil would protect her as best she could; he knew that. Elaine would likely be all right, unless her mother lost control of Caddo Jack.

The more time that passed, the more hopeful Gabe became about John. If John had avoided capture until dark, he had a

far better chance of getting away. And if Holzer and his men had run him down, Gabe knew he'd be one of the first to know. Holzer would come straight for him to crow about the news. He'd tell Gabe every detail of what had happened, of how John had died. If Holzer didn't find John, he'd do exactly as Keetch had predicted: He'd take out his frustration on Gabe. Maybe he'd shoot him on the spot. If he thought Lil wouldn't climb his back, he wouldn't think about it twice.

Gabe looked up at Keetch. Keetch had traded his broken chair by the door for a place before the dinner fire he had built in his small brick oven. Meat was heating up, and Keetch had something boiling that looked like mud and smelled like burning tar.

"What's that you've got there?" Gabe asked. "I'd appreciate a cup if you can spare it."

Keetch gave him a narrow look. "Shouldn't give you nothin' at all. You tried to get me in trouble is what you did."

"I made you an offer, Keetch. That's all. Nothing says you have to take it."

"I damn sure don't. And I ain't a'goin' to, either." Keetch pulled himself up and poured a cup of dark liquid in a cup. "This'll have to cool down," he said. "It's right hot."

"I'm not going anywhere," Gabe said.

Keetch grinned. "Now ain't that the truth?" He walked over to Gabe and squatted down by his head. "Thicket coffee ain't what you're likely used to in a town. Probably don't taste like what you get in Fort Worth."

"I guess you'll have to wonder about that."

"I 'spect I will," said Keetch. "Don't matter to me at all, either, if you're thinkin' that it does."

"Wasn't thinking about coffee. I kinda had my mind on a redheaded gal."

Keetch's eyes narrowed. "I told you, mister, I don't want to hear about that."

"Reckon I forgot."

"Well don't."

Past Keetch's shoulders, Gabe saw a figure appear in the door against the dark. He looked quickly back to Keetch.

"That stuff about cooled down?"

"I can give it to you scaldin' hot if you want," Keetch grumbled. "Don't make a damn to me if your burn your—huh!"

Keetch's eyes went blank. The cup dropped from his hand, and Keetch fell flat on his face.

John Marshall slapped a piece of oaken firewood against his palm and grinned at Gabe.

"Guess he spilled your drink," Marshall said. "I 'pologize for that."

"Don't," Gabe said. "Doubt if I missed a whole lot. Damn, I'm glad to see you, John. Look, pour some water on that fire real quick. We don't need a lot of light."

Marshall found a tin pot and doused the fire at once. Then he crawled behind Gabe and started slicing at his bonds.

"Heard you stole a boat," Gabe said.

"Did," Marshall said. "Took it out 'bout twenty feet and sunk it. Figured they'd think I was gone. Left enough sign for a blind man to see. Took the long way 'round back to here. Shoot, I been perched in a tree like a bird, waiting for the dark. Lord, mister, your hands and feet don't look real good at all."

The moment Marshall cut the ropes away, blood rushed into Gabe's limbs. He closed his eyes and shut out the pain, as the Lakota people had taught him. The hurt isn't there unless you let it. Don't accept it, shut it out.

"I'm sorry I waited so long," Marshall said solemnly.

"That's all right," Gabe said. "You did the right thing. You were right not to risk it in daylight."

"After you left me at the pens, I heard all the commotion going on and figured I better take a look. Saw you fightin' that crazy man and saw 'em take you off. How's everything feeling now?"

"Better," Gabe said. He vigorously rubbed his feet and hands. "I'd like to sit around here a couple of days, but I doubt we've got the time for that."

Marshall bound up Keetch, rolled him in a corner under a blanket, and forked a piece of meat from the fire. Gabe stood and tried to make his legs work right. He could shut out the pain, but he couldn't force the muscles to work the way they should. Only time would take care of that.

Marshall returned Gabe's knife and picked up his club. Gabe took a close look at Keetch's rifle in the half light and decided he'd been right the first time. The weapon would do more damage to the shooter than the target. Hefting up his pack, he led John Marshall outside into the dark.

Gabe was thankful for the celebration, whatever it was about. Nearly everyone in the settlement was gathered in the clearing near Lil's house. A big bonfire was burning, a fiddle band was playing, and there seemed to be plenty to drink for all. After one close call, Gabe and Marshall learned to look for couples who had sneaked out under a tree. This seemed to be the only danger, though Gabe kept his eyes open for men staggering off to urinate or throw up.

Trees and brush grew right up to the back of Lil's house. Vines trailed up from the ground and formed a thick curtain on the wall. Gabe could see faint light from a window, filtered through a tangle of heavy growth. While Marshall stood watch, Gabe cut his way through with his knife, working as quietly as he could. Pushing the vines aside, he found the window was covered with oiled paper. Gabe breathed a sigh of relief. There wasn't a glass window in the settlement, as far as he could tell, and he was grateful that Lil hadn't thought to buy this luxury for herself.

Squatting down low, Gabe cut a small slit in the paper, eased down the opening with the tip of his blade, and peered inside. He silently said another prayer. Elaine was sitting alone at the table. She stared at the wall, hands folded in her lap. Gabe widened the slit to get a view of the entire room. It was empty. No one else was there. Past Elaine, he could see the open door that led to the clearing. The bonfire blazed, casting distorted shadows as dancers hopped about to the fiddler's tune.

"Elaine," Gabe said quietly, "it's me, Gabe."

Elaine cried out, jerked around, and stared.

"No," Gabe said sharply, "sit down and don't turn around."

Elaine sat. "Gabe, where the hell are you? Will you please tell me that?"

"I'm here at the window. Now listen, Elaine. Get up slowly. Walk over here like you're just looking for something. Don't

look behind you. I can see the door fine."

Elaine nodded. She stood shakily, straightened her hair, and came toward Gabe.

"I can't see you," Elaine said. Gabe could read the apprehension in her eyes. "Are you all right, Gabe? They—they went after John. He got away and stole a boat."

"John's here with me. Now hang on a minute. I'm going to cut this window."

Gabe ran his knife along the bottom of the paper, then up both sides about a foot. He checked the door again and stuck the knife in his belt.

"Now, stick your hands and your head through the window. There, that's good. I'm going to grab your shoulders, Elaine, and pull you through."

"Gabe . . ."

"Take it easy. You'll be out of there in a second."

"My shirt's stuck, Gabe."

"Your shirt's what?"

"It's stuck on something; I don't know what."

"Well unstick it, Elaine, we don't have time to—"

Gabe froze. A bearded man suddenly stepped through the door, a crock in one hand, a tin cup in the other. He blinked in disbelief at the shapely bottom disappearing through the window. An instant after that he spotted Gabe, dropped the tin cup, and yanked a pistol from his belt.

Gabe grabbed Elaine's shoulders and pulled. The drunk cocked his pistol and fired. Dishes shattered on the wall. The weapon's barrel was waving everywhere. A shot thunked into wood. Another parted Gabe's hair.

"Gabe, I'm stuck," Elaine cried out. "God, my belt's caught on a nail!"

The drunk fired again. Lead plowed into the window not an inch from Elaine's head. Gabe shouted in anger and frustration. He knew what he had to do. Before he could change his mind, he shoved Elaine roughly into the room, out of the line of fire. The drunk emptied his gun at the window as Gabe threw himself into the brush, came to his feet, and ran.

John Marshall appeared in the dark, gripping his club. He stared curiously at Gabe.

"Where's Miss Elaine? What happened in there?"

"Come on, we haven't got the time," Gabe blurted out. He looked back once at the house, then led Marshall running back the way they'd come.

Gabe could hear men yelling behind him. Someone shot blindly into the dark. Gabe passed the rear of Keetch's house, ducked under a branch, and headed down the path he'd taken that afternoon. He figured their pursuers would head for the main dock first, expecting he and John to go there. They might not think of the spot on the end of the island where Gabe had seen the man guarding the other boats. They would come soon enough, but it would buy a little time.

Gabe had guessed there wouldn't be any guard this time, and he was right. He slid one of the slim pirogues off the mud, while John gathered up a pair of oars and launched as many boats as he could into the swamp.

Wading out from shore a few yards, Gabe crawled into the boat. John followed on his heels. Torches and lanterns were bobbing about on shore. Gabe turned away and thrust his oar into the water. The pirogue rushed swiftly into the dark. Shots echoed over the water, but Gabe didn't look back.

I had her, he thought, held her and nearly brought her out, and then I let her go—left her there with Holzer and Lil and Caddo Jack. Gabe could still see the look in her eyes when he'd thrust her back into the room. Christ, she didn't understand; she didn't know why. Gabe stared straight ahead and rowed, fighting back the fury that raged inside his head.

CHAPTER TWENTY-ONE

Gabe could hear them behind him, shouting to one another. Their torches and lanterns cast pools of yellow light on the water. The swampers had quit wasting shots in the dark, but Gabe told Marshall to keep his head low just in case. A lucky shot could kill you just as quickly as any other kind.

"If you've got any idea where we are," Gabe said quietly, "I'd sure be pleased to hear it."

"Keetch brung us in here down that channel to your right," Marshall said. "Might be they'll figure that's where we'll try and go."

"Good a plan as any," Gabe said. He shifted his knees in the bow and angled the pirogue to the left. The way ahead was thick with cypress trees bearded with Spanish moss. Gabe rowed another few yards, glanced over his shoulder, and guided the boat to cover beneath the moss.

Marshall leaned forward. "Lord, what we stoppin' here for?" he asked anxiously. "Them fellas is right behind us, Mister Gabe."

"We can't outrun 'em," Gabe said. "They can take turns rowing, and we can't. I'm thinking we might try and let them

get ahead. They can't search every damn tree in the dark."

"Might work," Marshall said, though he didn't sound all that certain to Gabe.

Gabe took another look through the moss and eased down close to Marshall. "I didn't have time to talk back there," he said. "I want you to know what happened. If I'd tried to pull her out of that window, that drunk might've got her in the back. I had to leave her, John. There wasn't anything else I could do."

Marshall nodded. "You did what you could. I'm right certain of that."

"If anything happens to Elaine because I messed it up . . ."

Marshall gripped Gabe's shoulder hard. "Wasn't anything else you could do. We'll get her back; you know we're going to do that."

Gabe didn't answer. He didn't have the slightest idea how they'd manage to set Elaine free. At the moment, they seemed to be headed the wrong way.

"Somethin' you ought to know," Marshall said. "While I was hidin' out in that tree, I heard a couple of those fellas talking. One of 'em just come back from a raid with that Caddo Jack. Couldn't hear much, but he was braggin' 'bout all the guns and horses they got."

Gabe stared at Marshall. He felt something cold knot up in his belly. "That's what the big celebration was about, then. If Caddo Jack got guns and horses somewhere, you can bet they're for that army you spotted on the island across from the settlement."

Gabe frowned thoughtfully into the dark. "We knew they were up to something. Now we know they've got the arms and the mounts they need. Only thing we don't know is what they intend to use 'em for."

"Nothing good," Marshall said. "Goin' to cause a lot of trouble for someone, you can bet your last dollar on that."

Gabe touched Marshall's arm and nodded to his left. Marshall went silent at once. Through the moss, they could see the first boats gliding slowly through the trees. Gabe watched them pass and counted fourteen boats in all. Each held three or four men. At least one man in each boat carried a lantern or a torch, and

Gabe was sure they would all have shotguns or rifles. The pursuers were silent now; there was no more shouting across the water. They knew they'd lost their prey for the moment, and they were taking no chances on missing the slightest sound in the dark.

"They did like we figured," Marshall whispered. "They took off to the right."

Gabe didn't answer. Marshall's words did little to reassure him. They were safe for the moment, but that didn't mean a thing. The men from the settlement had been born and raised in the Thicket. The night might hamper their search, but not for long. They knew every inch of the swamp in the daylight or the dark. Darkness might delay them for a while, but when the sun came up again . . .

"Let's go," Gabe said finally. "I don't know where that left-hand channel goes, but it beats tailing after that bunch."

The channel to the left was shallow and narrow, sheltered by willows and ancient oaks. Gabe and Marshall rowed silently through seemingly endless lagoons strangled with weeds and rotting wood. Once, Gabe heard a grunt and saw a giant gator slide off the flats and into the water less than ten feet away.

The land seemed fairly solid on either side, thick with trees and tangled vines. Probably a snake or two every square foot, Gabe thought. Maybe three or four.

Peering through the night, he could see the channel ahead was choked with weeds. He raised a hand to signal Marshall and quickly back-rowed the pirogue to a halt.

"Don't know if we can get through that or not," Gabe said softly. "If we do, we're going to make a hell of a lot of noise. That stuff looks brittle as tinder."

Marshall nodded. "It's either that or go back."

"I don't think we want to try that. And I sure don't want to stay here." Gabe stopped and listened to the night. There was nothing but the dry rattle of locusts and the distant call of an owl.

"I think what we'll do is pull up to that brush and take a look," Gabe said. "If it seems like we can make it, we'll

give her a try. If it doesn't look right, we'll try something else."

"Like goin' back," Marshall said.

"Yeah, maybe like going back. I don't like it any more than you do, but we—"

Gabe froze. A sharp, deep sound carried over the night air.

Marshall stared at Gabe. "That wasn't no gator," he whispered.

"I know what it was," Gabe said. "It was one of our friends trying to hold off a cough." He felt the hackles rise on the back of his neck. If they hadn't stopped, he was certain they would never have heard the sound. They would have rowed right into a trap.

"They're waiting for us over there. Probably split up, sent a bunch on ahead, and left a couple of boats here. Someone figured we might try the other way."

"We goin' back?"

Gabe shook his head. He tried to picture the water and the terrain he couldn't see. There was land on either side, the brushy channel between the two boggy islands. The men were waiting behind the brush. Gabe was damned and determined not to go back. It would take a lot of time, and by now the swampers might have another boat or two waiting near the entry to the settlement. He studied the tangled island to his left.

"Turn around slow and easy," he said finally. "Head over there."

Marshall frowned in the dark. "Don't look like a real good place to me."

"Neither is this," Gabe told him. "Let's go."

Gabe took the lead, carrying the prow of the boat while Marshall took the stern. The island was thick with second growth willow, vines, and cutting thorns. He took it slow, one step at a time, praying he wouldn't step on something that would make a loud noise. He tried not to think about snakes. Maybe, he reasoned, the snakes wouldn't think about him.

God, how big was the damn island? He decided they'd gone twenty yards or maybe more. Something black slithered off through the grass. Gabe stopped, waited, then took another cautious step ahead. His boot sank six inches deep in water.

Gabe breathed a silent sigh of relief and carefully lowered the front of the pirogue into the swamp. Marshall came up beside him. Gabe held the boat steady while Marshall got in, then crawled aboard himself.

Thirty yards ahead, thick weeds and tall saplings trailed off the end of the island, forming a barrier parallel to the land. If I'm right, Gabe thought, the swampers are waiting some ways to the right, beyond the stand of brush blocking the channel we just left.

He leaned over and gathered as many chunks of rotten wood as he could find and set them gently in the bottom of the boat. Nodding to Marshall, he started rowing toward the heavy line of weeds. When the end of the island was fifteen or twenty feet ahead, he pulled the pirogue to a stop, leaned back, and whispered his instructions. Marshall nodded, understanding, and hefted some good-sized chunks of wood.

"All right, *now!*" Gabe whispered.

Together, they started tossing chunks across the island, aiming for the channel where they'd been. Gabe had hurled two when gunfire shattered the night.

Gabe raised his hand, and Marshall stopped. The swampers whooped victory yells and fired off their weapons. Gabe could hear their boats cracking dry brush as they paddled swiftly into the empty channel.

Gabe grinned and turned to Marshall. "It won't take 'em long to find out we're not there. Let's get the hell out of here, friend."

"Don't have to ask me twice," Marshall said.

Dawn broke through the thick canopy of trees overhead. Feeble shafts of light, pale as butter, spotted the dark waters of the swamp. As ever, morning turned the Thicket into a furnace. The last of the night air sizzled into steam, waking a billion mosquitoes into activity.

Gabe wondered where the hell they were now. The position of the sun told him they were going due west. So what? Gabe thought. Knowing which way you were headed had little to do with where you were.

At least, they'd lost their pursuers in the night. They might be just behind, around the last bend, but for the moment they weren't in sight.

"Anything look familiar to you?" Gabe asked.

"Shoot, everything does," Marshall said solemnly.

"Yeah, me too."

They were sitting in the pirogue near the shore, under the shade of a cypress tree. The water was deep and nearly clear for a change, the mouth of a creek that flowed into a marshy lake ahead. Gabe felt as if they'd been this way before, but he couldn't be sure. As John Marshall said, everything looked pretty much the same in the Thicket.

During the night, Gabe had done his best to keep track of the way they'd come. While he didn't know exactly where they were, he was certain he could find his way back to the settlement and Elaine. All I need is a weapon, something to eat and drink, and a couple of dozen men, he thought grimly. What I've got is me and John and a pair of oars.

"Robert Porter's posse was headed southwest when we saw 'em," Gabe said. "I'm thinking we came this far and maybe a little east before we spotted those riders. I'm not dead sure, you understand, but that's what I think. We can angle off south and try to find them. There's dry land over there, and we've got a good chance of picking up their trail."

"If they haven't turned back," Marshall said, "or gone off some other way."

"Right," Gabe agreed, "but I don't see we've got a lot of choice. Besides, I wouldn't mind getting out of this boat. They won't spot us near as well if we're on dry land. You got any objections?"

"None I can think of right off," Marshall said.

Gabe nodded, then guided the boat down the creek toward the broad, marshy lake. Past the thick swamp grass, the way ahead was clear. The dead, skeletal trees in the lake looked familiar, and Gabe felt a sudden surge of hope. If that was so,

they were on the right track. They could beach the pirogue across the lake, go ashore, and look for the tracks of Porter's outfit.

"John, I'm thinking we've been here before. What do you think?"

"I'm thinking the same thing." Marshall laughed softly. "I'm thinking we're maybe not lost. We ain't exactly *found*, but we maybe got us a start."

Gabe started to speak. A flock of white herons suddenly erupted from the edge of the lake, squawking loudly and scattering above the trees.

Gabe sat up straight and squinted across the water. Something made them rise, he thought. Something scared them off, and it wasn't us.

"John, let's get going," he said shortly. "Row like hell for shore. Over there!"

"What's wrong?" Marshall asked. "Don't see any—"

The shot rang out across the water, a flat, ugly sound that seemed to go on forever. Marshall cried out, threw his oar in the air, and jerked to one side of the boat. Gabe tried to keep the pirogue steady, but the narrow craft tilted at once.

Gabe hit the water, came up fast, and searched about for Marshall. Marshall was nowhere in sight. Lead chunked into the overturned boat by Gabe's head. Gabe ducked under again, swam beneath the boat, and poked his head up on the other side. Marshall was five feet away, floating on his face.

Gabe went to him quickly, turning him over, and raising his head above the water. Marshall's face was covered with blood. He choked once, stared at Gabe, and then closed his eyes.

"Damn it, you better not die on me now," Gabe said under his breath. "By God, I won't have you doing that!"

Grasping Marshall's head in the crook of his arm, Gabe started swimming for the shore. He couldn't see where the shots had come from. Behind the boat, maybe near the shore somewhere.

Twenty, thirty yards, I ought to be able to do that. Just keep going, don't stop. Keep going and you'll make it just fine.

Someone laughed. Gabe jerked around and stared, saw the boat coming at him, not forty feet away. There were three

gaunt, heavily bearded swampers in the boat. The man in the bow was on his knees. He held a rifle against his shoulder, and Gabe could look right down the dark and ugly muzzle of the gun.

"Shit, Billy," the man in the stern complained. "I ought to get to kill the other one. That ain't hardly fair."

"Fair, my ass." The man called Billy grinned. "I'm a'goin' to shoot me some dark and white meat both, all at one sittin'!"

CHAPTER TWENTY-TWO

The man in the boat levered a shell into his rifle and closed one eye. Gabe felt strangely calm, as if he played no part in this at all. There was nothing he could say, nothing he could do to save his life. He wasn't even angry anymore. There was no time left for such emotions as anger or regret.

John Marshall groaned in Gabe's arms. He thrashed about and rolled his eyes. The man named Billy stared in disbelief and lowered the rifle from his cheek.

The two men behind Billy laughed. "Real nice shootin'," one said. "Sumbitch ain't even dead."

"Can't wait to tell your ol' daddy you had to kill somebody twice," said the other.

"Shut yer mouth," Billy yelled. "He's goin' to be dead soon enough. Him and the white feller, too!"

"Might be I ought to row closer?" The man in the stern grinned. "Don't want to take no chance on you missing again."

Billy muttered under his breath, raised the rifle again, and aimed at Gabe's head. Gabe heard the loud report. He jerked back, squeezed his eyes shut, then opened them again, startled to find he was still alive.

Billy tumbled headfirst into the water. The man in the stern shouted something to his friend. Two quick shots followed the first. One of the men cried out and collapsed in the boat. The other, the swamper in the stern, managed to grab his shotgun before he died.

Gabe stared at the shore to his left. A tall, rawboned man in a straw hat eased himself down from his horse, set the rifle by a tree, and started wading into the swamp.

"Harper?" Gabe could scarcely believe his eyes. "By God, I never expected to be glad to see you."

"Don't get all worked up," Harper said tightly. "I ain't real pleased to see you either, Conrad." He reached Gabe, frowned, and looked at Marshall. "Christ, that's John, ain't it? Is he dead?"

"Got creased pretty good, but I reckon he'll be all right."

Gabe found his pack floating nearby and hauled it in. Harper carried Marshall ashore.

"He's goin' to make it fine," Harper said. "I expect he'll have one hell of a headache for a while." He found a bandanna in his pocket and wrapped it around Marshall's head.

Gabe sat down on dry grass and poured water out of his boots. The two boats were still afloat, bobbing toward the shore. Gabe saw one body, but couldn't spot the other two.

"Bastards would've killed us both if they hadn't started arguing over marksmanship," Gabe said. "What were you doing, waiting to see if he missed?"

"Get up," Harper said.

"What?" Gabe looked up to see the sheriff towering over him, hands on his hips.

"I said get up, damn you!"

Gabe stood. He made it halfway before Harper caught him solidly on the jaw and sent him sprawling.

Gabe came to his feet, shook his head, and worked his jaw. "Now what the hell was that for?"

" 'Cause I felt like it's why. Where's Elaine? By God, she better be all right. If she's not, mister, if something's happened to her . . ."

Harper took a step toward Gabe, fists doubled at his sides.

"All right, just hold it," Gabe said, raising up his hands.

"You want to fight or you want to listen? I'm willing to take you on, but we can't do both at once."

"I'm listening," Harper said darkly. "I better hear something soon."

As quickly as he could, Gabe filled Harper in on everything that had happened, including Elaine's "kidnapping" scheme, but leaving out the lovemaking at the Excelsior Hotel. He told Harper about Holzer, Lil, and Caddo Jack, and the army Lil had gathered. Harper raised a brow at Lil's story about Porter blaming his brother Josh for the rape of the Indian girl.

"I maybe believe that or not," Harper said. "Don't much matter if I do or if I don't. I know the part about the half-breed's raid is true. He got a bunch of horses and guns two days ago, south of Woodville. Killed 'bout nine people doin' it, too."

Harper stared out across the swamp. "Porter's got half the men in East Texas out here lookin' for his daughter. Since the Woodville raid, the other half's ridin' in, too. Shit, we got near two hundred men out stirring up snakes."

Gabe let out a breath. "Lil's got something going, I just don't know what. She's crazy as a tick, Harper, but she's not a stupid woman. She's figured every bit of this right from the start. Getting Porter's brother up to Jefferson to kill him, and then having Caddo Jack murder the Clays. It's all part of getting back at Robert Porter. That's the whole thing." Gabe paused. "And this army of hers she's got going, everything's working just the way she wants it to. She's drawn every able man in here to the Thicket. That bunch of hers is going to hit somewhere, and when they do, nobody's going to be around to stop 'em."

"I got to say it all fits," Harper admitted. "Hell, I hate to admit it, but the whole business makes a lot of sense."

Gabe looked squarely at Harper. "We've got to stop Lil's folks, and we've got to get Elaine out of there. Neither one of those jobs is going to be real easy."

"We've got plenty of riders," Harper said. "We'll get it done."

"Fine," Gabe said sourly, "only you've got no idea what to do with them. Lil's boys know every cottonmouth snake in the

Thicket by its first name. We can't stop 'em if we can't even find them, Harper."

"We'll find them, and we'll stop 'em," Harper said shortly. "We got some ol' boys with us that know the swamp as well as Lil's crew." Harper squinted at the sun. "We better be gettin' on back. I want Mr. Porter to hear all this."

Gabe stood his ground. "You and me aren't ever going to be best friends, but I figure you've got a good head on your shoulders. You send a couple of hundred men in there shootin' everything that moves, you aren't going to find anybody, and you're likely to get Elaine killed. That's not the way to do it, and you know it!"

Harper's eyes went dark. He drew his gun and stepped back from Gabe. "That isn't your concern anymore. You're flat out of it, mister."

"I'm damned if I am," Gabe bristled.

"Get John up on my horse," Harper said. "We've got a good hour's walking to do."

Robert Porter had set up camp in a grove of oak trees. Gabe told him everything he'd told Harper, leaving out Lil's version of the rape. By the time he was finished, Porter's face was red with rage. Jake Harper had to wrestle a shotgun from him and pin him against a tree.

"Mr. Porter, now you don't want to kill no one," Harper said calmly. "That isn't going to help anything. It isn't going to get Elaine back any quicker."

"He's got her!" Porter shouted hoarsely, shaking a fist at Gabe. "He's got her hidden somewhere if he hasn't already given her to that—that savage!" He gave Harper a wild-eyed look. "By God, Jake, I didn't take you for a fool. Don't you see what he's doing? He's in with those swampers. He's a part of all this!"

"I don't like him a lot, Mr. Porter, but I don't believe that," Harper said. "I think what he's telling us is true."

Porter stared. Finally, his face split into a terrible grin. "Are you in this too, Jake? Is that it? What did they do, buy you off?"

Harper gave Porter a chilling look. "You've got no call to

say that, Mr. Porter. I won't stand here and listen to that."

"You're wasting a lot of time, both of you," Gabe said irritably. "You want to stand and yell at each other, or you want to help Elaine?"

"Stay out of this," Harper warned.

"Like hell I will."

"Get him out of here!" Porter yelled, pointing a shaky finger at Gabe. "Get him out, or I swear I'll kill him, Jake!"

Gabe started to speak, but Harper shoved him roughly down the path, out of Porter's sight. When they were well out of the trees, Gabe stopped and turned on Harper.

"Seems you forgot to mention the man's a flat-out lunatic," he said evenly. "Harper, if he's running this show, Elaine's as good as dead."

"He isn't acting real normal, you're right about that."

"My God, he isn't even close."

"Just shut up, Conrad, all right?" He rammed the pistol in Gabe's back. "The more you talk, the more aggravated I get."

Harper led Gabe through the camp toward the shore of the swamp. There were men and horses everywhere, scattered about among the trees and the clearing by the water. Gabe saw a patrol riding out and another coming back. Riders scurried about like angry bees disturbed in a hive. If there was any kind of order to Porter's expedition, Gabe couldn't see it. Everyone's real busy, he thought, but no one's getting anything done.

John Marshall was resting beneath a tree, a clean bandage circled about his head. A guard stood nearby with a rifle. Marshall looked up and grinned as Gabe approached.

"You feeling all right?" Gabe asked. "You're looking real spry, John."

"Spry ain't exactly how I'd put it," Marshall said. "Don't guess I'm dead, either."

"Glad to see you sittin' up," Harper said. He motioned Gabe to sit, then called out to the guard. "You can get some coffee, Mack. I'll call you if I need you."

The guard nodded and walked off. Harper looked narrowly

at Gabe. "I want your word," he said. "Don't like to say it, but I figure that it's good. Am I right about that or not?"

"If I give it to you, it's good," Gabe said.

Harper seemed satisfied with that. "I'm asking you, Conrad, and you too, John. I want to know if everything you've told me is the truth. Everything that happened out there, including the part about Elaine."

"If that's what you're asking, yes. You've got my word on it."

"Mine too, Mr. Harper," Marshall said.

Harper frowned thoughtfully, nodded to himself, and stood. "All right, then. I had to know that."

"Mind telling me what you're asking for?" Gabe said.

Harper didn't answer. He turned and stalked off up the hill. In a moment, the guard came back, sat down on a log, and rolled a smoke.

"What you reckon that was all about?" Marshall said.

"I've quit trying to figure the man," Gabe muttered. "Half the time he's thinking straight, and half the time he's not."

"How's Mr. Porter?"

"Mr. Porter's about that close to foaming at the mouth," Gabe said. "He's got this posse of his runnin' around in circles, and he's plain scared to death." Gabe shook his head. "Lil's got him hopping, just like she figured she would. Couldn't be working out any better."

"So what are we going to do, just sit here and do nothing?" Marshall glanced at the guard and leaned in close to Gabe. "If I was to start in groanin' and rollin' about, that fella might come in close. If you was to jump him . . ."

"Forget it. He doesn't look like a man wants to get himself jumped. Get some rest, John. That's what I'm going to do."

Marshall frowned. "Don't seem right. Not doing anything to help Miss Elaine."

"It's not," Gabe said, "but that's what we're going to do anyway." He stretched out under the tree, tipped his hat up over his face, and went to sleep.

Gabe figured a couple of hours had passed when Marshall nudged him awake. Gabe sat up and saw Jake Harper coming

Snaketown

toward them down the hill. Harper stopped and spoke to the guard. The man stood and walked away.

Harper looked down at Gabe and Marshall. "You boys get rested up good?"

"Real kind of you to ask," Gabe said.

"Get on your feet," Harper snapped. "We're going to take a walk."

"This where we get fed to the gators?" Gabe asked.

"How'd you guess?"

"Sorta came to me," Gabe said.

Harper guided them along the shore to the south of the camp through swamp grass and a stand of second growth. The saplings gave way to a grove of cypress trees that marched from the shore out into the shallows.

Harper stopped, led them down a steep bank, and pulled a tangle of vines aside.

Gabe saw a long pirogue at the edge of the water. His pack was in the boat, along with a small cache of supplies, canteens of water, and three Winchester rifles.

Gabe repressed a grin. "Now you've hurt my feelings, Harper. Looks to me like you don't want me and John around."

"Just get in the damn boat," Harper growled. "Isn't any need for talk." He paused and looked soberly at Gabe. "You think you can find your way back to that place where they're keepin' Elaine?"

"Me and John between us can try."

"Let's get at it, then," Harper said. "We're wasting a lot of time."

"That's what I told you before."

"And I told you to shut up," Harper said.

CHAPTER TWENTY-THREE

They sat in the pirogue under a stand of water oak. There was still an hour of sunlight left above the trees, but night already had a gloomy hold on the Thicket. Gabe studied the dock of the settlement through Harper's binoculars, then passed them back to the sheriff.

"I don't see a damn thing," Harper said. "Where the hell is everybody?"

"They're gone," Gabe said. He felt a cold emptiness in the pit of his stomach. "I expect there's a few old men hanging 'round, but the rest of them are gone."

"Jesus Christ." Harper looked at Gabe. The meaning of his words was all too clear. Wherever Lil's army was headed, they were already well on the way.

"Let's go," Gabe said. "I know a spot up the way where we can land without being spotted. No use taking any chances."

John Marshall rowed while Gabe and Jake Harper studied the shore, rifles at the ready. Leaving the boat at the tip of the island, they made their way cautiously down the pathway to the settlement.

The first two shacks were deserted. There were still warm ashes in the cooking fires, but no one was around. The next

five houses held women and children. When Gabe, Marshall, and Harper appeared, the people backed away and cowered, their gaunt faces taut with fear.

Gabe peered into Keetch's house and found it empty as well. At the last house before the clearing, an old man poked his head around the corner, saw the strangers, and ran for the woods.

Harper raised his rifle, but Gabe shook his head. "Let him go," he said. "He isn't going to do us any harm."

Lil's house was deserted. Everything was scattered about, as if someone had left in a hurry. Gabe looked for signs of Elaine—some of her belongings, a shirt, a shoe, anything at all—as if some trace of her might somehow assure him she was still all right.

Harper caught Gabe's expression. "This is where they kept her?"

"Yes," Gabe said, "this is where she was."

"You said the mother, this Lil, you said she'd keep her safe. You still believe that?"

"I believe she'll try."

Harper nodded but didn't speak. Gabe looked about the room once more. There wasn't a lot to see. He was holding a broken whiskey crock when three quick shots sounded outside the hut. Gabe ran out behind Harper in time to see Marshall squeeze off another round into the trees.

"Couple of leftovers," Marshall said. "Came out to see who we was."

"They armed?" Harper asked.

"One of 'em was. Had him an ol' shotgun."

"They won't bother us," Gabe said. "Just keep your eyes open."

Past the hog pens where John Marshall had worked, they found a flat-bottomed boat and rowed across to the spot where Marshall had seen Lil's men gathering. There were dead fires and plenty of signs that men and horses had been there, but nothing else.

"We're a little late," Harper said angrily, stomping about the clearing. "We can follow their trail easy, but that won't do a hell of a lot of good."

"Not walking it won't," Gabe said.

"You got any good ideas?"

"Get word back to Porter's bunch. See if we can convince him to get off his ass."

"Fat chance of that," Harper said bitterly. "Reason I came with you is I knew that old bastard was getting crazier by the minute. He sure ain't likely to listen to me now."

"Might or might not. Depends if he still recalls what he came out here for."

"Mister Gabe," Marshall called out, "over here—quick!"

Gabe and Harper ran toward Marshall. He was standing by a big live oak, staring wide-eyed at something on the ground.

"Aw, hell," Gabe said. "Damn those sons of bitches!" He pounded his fist against his side, fighting back the cold rage that surged through his veins.

Keetch was staked out naked on the ground, spread-eagled, facedown. The flesh from his back to his feet was flayed raw, nearly to the bone. A great cloud of blue flies swarmed up as Gabe bent down and raised the man's head.

"Keetch, it's me, Gabe Conrad. Talk to me if you can."

Keetch groaned, opened one eye, and tried to grin. "Guess I—shoulda gone with you," he said weakly. "Sure would've liked to—meet that redheaded gal."

Marshall handed Gabe a canteen. Gabe offered Keetch a drink, but Keetch shook his head.

"We'll go see her," Gabe said gently. "You and me. That's a promise, Keetch."

Keetch tried to laugh. The effort screwed up his face in pain. "Yeah, we'll—do that sometime."

"Keetch, I'm sorry 'bout this, but I got to ask. You know where they were headed? Lil's men. Where were they going, Keetch, can you say?"

Keetch's lips moved, but Gabe couldn't hear. He swatted flies away and leaned in close.

"North," Keetch mumbled. "Goin' up—north."

"*Where* up north? Can you tell me where? Keetch? Keetch!"

Gabe heard a last breath sigh from Keetch's lips. Almost at once, the familiar glaze of death veiled his eyes.

Snaketown

Gabe stood. "North," he said tightly. "That doesn't tell us a lot. Damn it all!" He slammed a fist against his palm. "They did this to him 'cause he let me get away. Most likely, Caddo Jack did the honors himself. It's the kind of thing he likes to do. See if you can find me a shovel or something, will you, John? Least I can do is lay this fella in the ground, seein' as how it was me that put him there."

"Don't go blamin' yourself," Harper said.

Gabe turned on the man and glared. "Yeah? Who would you like to blame? Only decent man I met in this hole, and they killed him. Someone's going to pay for Keetch. Caddo Jack's running up a score with me."

Marshall got a fire going and rummaged through Harper's supplies to find something for a meal. Night had closed in by the time Gabe buried Keetch and walked down to the water to wash up. When Gabe returned, Harper handed him a cup of coffee and spread out a map before the fire.

"This isn't a real good chart of the Thicket," he said, " 'cause there hasn't been a lot of mappin' done. I picked it up in Porter's tent before I left. Look right here." He pointed. "If they took off north like Keetch said, that'd take 'em past Flat Cypress Creek up by Honey Island. If this map makes any sense, this island we're on isn't an island at all. It thins out but stays dry and goes all the way north on solid ground. Now Porter's bunch is over near Old Bragg Road. At least I think they are. Sorta north of Saratoga. Should be a straight shot west of here. A lot faster than the way we came today."

Gabe frowned at the map. "So if we follow Lil's trail, we ought to keep dry at least. We'll have to find ourselves some mounts somewhere. Walking isn't going to cut it, going after that bunch."

Gabe turned to Marshall and showed him where they were looking. "I'm going to ask you to do this, John, if you're willing. I'd like you to take a pirogue and cut across here." Gabe jabbed a finger at the map. "With any luck, you ought to run into Porter and his bunch. In about half the time it took us to get here."

Marshall studied the map. "I can do it, all right. Don't know what Mr. Porter'll do when he sees me. Doubt if he's real happy with *me*, either."

Harper shook his head. "Don't go to him. See a man named Nat Kramer. He's a lawman from Hardin County, a friend of mine, and a man with good sense. Go straight to him and tell him I sent you. Tell him we figure with the start they had, Lil's bunch ought to be about—what? A little north of Village Mills. If that's the way they went, of course. If they didn't, we're shit out of luck."

"I'll get there," Marshall said. "Travelin' in the dark's better than doin' it in daylight. Less chance of seein' folks you don't want to meet."

After supper, Gabe and Harper shook hands with John Marshall and wished him luck. Marshall got himself some supplies, a canteen, and one of the Winchester rifles. Gabe walked with him down to the shore.

"You take care," Gabe told him. "I'm not aiming to lose you again."

Marshall looked at Gabe a long moment. "You find Miss Elaine. You get her back safe."

"I will," Gabe said.

"Then I won't worry no more," Marshall said and disappeared into the dark.

The old man clearly didn't care much for strangers and wasn't about to sell two fine horses—especially to men who obviously didn't belong in the Thicket. Harper got impatient and told the old man he was an ornery son of a bitch and likely wanted by the law somewhere. This drove the price up considerably, and Gabe ended up paying three times what the worn-out nags were worth.

"Still say there's a poster out on that bastard," Harper grumbled. "Bet I got his picture in my office somewhere."

"Fine," Gabe said. "When this is all over, you come on back and take him in. Give you something to pass the time."

Harper swelled up like a toad. "By God, Conrad, I don't need nothin' to pass the time, if that's what you're trying to say. It's a full day's work, seven days a week, keeping law and

order in Jefferson, Texas. Sometimes you hardly get a chance to sit down for supper."

"Yeah, I guess so," Gabe said. "There's all those squirrels stealin' nuts off of rich folks' lawns. Someone's got to watch out for that. And those herons eating corn all the time."

Harper stared at Gabe. "When this is all over, you and me are going to finish up some business between us, Conrad. We sure as hell are."

"Lookin' forward to it," Gabe grinned. "I haven't wrestled a sheriff in some time."

Harper cursed under his breath.

The noonday sun blazed down from the washed-out summer sky. Water oak and willow had disappeared, replaced by forests of live oak and an occasional pine. Gabe found Lil's band easy enough to follow. The ground was damp, and a three-year-old Lakota boy could have read the signs clear in his sleep. The war party was moving fast, eating up the miles, and Harper was concerned about that. Gabe assured him this was all to the good. The harder the pace, the sooner they'd have to stop and rest the horses. He was sure they wouldn't have the luxury of extra mounts.

"We find 'em, then what?" Harper said. "You and me walk in and gun 'em all down?"

"Doesn't sound like a good idea," Gabe said. "I think I'd rather wait for Porter's men."

"Then you might be waiting till next winter," Harper said. He wiped sweat from his face and scowled. "Even if John finds 'em, someone's got to talk sense into Porter. I should've told John to tell my friend Nat Kramer to just knock the old man in the head. That'd be the quickest way to set things straight."

"John's a good man, the best there is," Gabe said. "He'll get there, all right. Hard to say what'll happen after that. Hope this friend of yours is as smart as you think."

Gabe looked past Harper into the trees ahead. The oaks thinned out past a slight rise in the land, giving way to open ground.

"I'm not real worried 'bout Porter's men," he said. "Mainly because they'll get here or they won't. I want to get Elaine out of there, Harper. That comes first. The closer Caddo Jack

gets to where it is he's going, the more he's going to start tasting blood. He's crazy as a loon right now. Lil thinks she can handle him, but she can't. Holzer keeps his eye on Caddo Jack all the time, but that killer's smart as a snake. If Caddo Jack goes after him, Holzer'll be holding his guts in his hand before he can blink. And if that maniac takes a mind to go after Elaine . . ."

Harper's jaw fell. "Jesus, Conrad, you ain't paintin' a real pretty picture. Things don't have to work out like that."

"They don't have to," Gabe said soberly, "but I'm sure worried that they might."

CHAPTER TWENTY-FOUR

Pine trees lined the slope of the low hill. The camp was in a hollow between the base of the hill and a shallow creek to the west. The horses were penned in a rope corral near the water. The swampers had picked a good spot. Except for the clearing itself, the area was thickly wooded; chances were slim that anyone would walk through the tangle of trees and stumble upon the camp.

Gabe sat at the base of a dead tree on the northeastern slope of the hill. Earlier in the night, cooking fires had dotted the hollow. Now, nearly everyone was bedded down. Only a few guards walked about. The whole place was dark except for watch fires at each end of the camp.

The cooking fires had tipped Gabe off. He smelled the camp long before he saw it. That had been close to ten o'clock, nearly six hours before. Gabe and Harper had walked and led their horses after dark, stopping now and then to squat down and feel the earth, to make certain the trail was still there. A torch would have helped, but they couldn't risk the light. Lil's bunch could be miles ahead or a few yards away in the night. Then Gabe smelled smoke and roasting meat and knew the search had come to an end. Circling far off to the east, they

came in through the woods and saw the fires down below.

The hard part was waiting. Gabe knew he didn't have a chance in hell of finding Elaine in the dark. Still, it was torture just sitting there, knowing she was down in the camp and that Caddo Jack was there, too. His gut said go down and get her somehow. Another minute, another hour, might be too late for Elaine. Reason said wait, and it took all the hard lessons of patience he had learned from the Lakotas to do that.

Gabe heard Jake Harper coming up behind him through the trees.

"You sleep any?" Gabe said, without taking his eyes off the clearing.

"Not a damn bit," Harper said. "What time you figure it is?"

Gabe looked up at the clear night sky. "Little after four, I'd say. We've got some time before the sun, Harper. I'm going to work my way down there in a minute, get as close as I can before it's light."

Harper was silent a long moment. "Any reason you think it ought to be you goin' in and not me? I don't recall taking any vote."

"It's me because I'm better at doing this," Gabe said evenly. "That isn't anything against you; it's just the truth. You're real handy with that Winchester, and I'll feel right comfortable knowing you're coverin' my tail. That suit you all right?"

"Yeah, I guess it does," Harper said. He looked soberly at Gabe and stuck out his hand. "Never thought I'd be wishing you luck, but I am."

Gabe grinned and met the man's grip. "Things don't always work out the way you figure, and that's a fact."

Gabe lay flat on his belly in a heavy thicket of fern. The foliage was wet with dew, and he was soaked through to the skin. The first dull hint of dawn touched the tops of the thick pine forest at his back. Now he could see the faint outlines of men bedded down, dark forms against the half light. A man coughed and rolled over in his blankets. Another rose sleepily, walked into the woods to relieve himself, than staggered back to camp. There were still guards about, but Gabe wasn't overly concerned. Several had quit their posts to sleep, and the rest were

simply passing the time till daylight and a hot cup of coffee.

It's a good time, Gabe thought. The world sleeps soundly just before the dawn. The Lakota had taught him that, too. It was the hour when children were born and men died.

The light was good enough now to see faces, to pick out the horses in the southwest corner of the hollow near the creek. The camp was beginning to stir. Two men rose and started building cooking fires. Another stood and stretched, scratched his belly, and yawned.

And then Gabe saw her. She sat up and ran her hands through her hair, not thirty yards down the hill. Almost at once, Lil sat up beside her. Probably been awake for a while, Gabe decided, waiting for Elaine.

Both women stood, talked for a moment, then started for the creek. Gabe came quickly to his knees, tracing a route with his eyes from his cover to the creek. He could keep to the edge of the trees where they circled up north then curled in toward the water. If he could make it over there, catch Elaine and her mother alone, he could gag Lil and have them back in the woods before anyone was the wiser. Because Elaine wouldn't leave without her mother. Harper would see his move and guess what he was doing. He would cover them with the Winchester, wait till they were clear, then circle around quickly with the horses.

"If I can get those mounts running through that tangle over there," Gabe muttered to himself, "won't any of those bastards get close."

Gabe touched his waist to make sure the knife stuck behind his belt was still there, then he came up slowly, ready to move out. Something moved in the woods to his right. A powerfully built man in buckskin pants and no shirt stomped into the clearing and headed for Lil and Elaine.

Gabe froze and sucked in a breath. It was Caddo Jack! He must have been sleeping in the trees off by himself, Gabe decided, sleeping no more than thirty feet from Gabe's cover all the time.

The hackles rose on the back of Gabe's neck. I could've crawled over and cut his throat, Gabe thought. Or he could've done the same to me.

Caddo Jack stalked up to Elaine and her mother. Elaine turned and saw him. She raised a hand to her throat, and Gabe could read the fear in her eyes. Lil stepped between them, set her hands on her hips, and stood her ground. Gabe couldn't hear what she said, but it was clear she was telling Caddo Jack off, warning him away.

Caddo Jack laughed in her face. He grabbed Elaine's arm, shoved her roughly to the ground, then turned on Lil. He pointed toward the creek. Even at a distance, the message was clear to Gabe. Lil could go, but Elaine would stay there.

Lil hesitated, trying to stare the man down. Caddo Jack took a step forward, raised his left arm, and slapped Lil with the back of his hand. Lil swayed, nearly lost her balance, and brought her hands quickly to her face. Then she turned and ran for the creek. Caddo Jack scowled down at Elaine, then walked off in the direction of the corral.

Gabe took a deep breath, held it, and closed his eyes. As the air escaped slowly through his lips, he willed the tension to leave him and set him free of anger. In a moment, he felt the life force, the *ni*, bring new calmness and strength to his body. He was Long Rider of the Lakota, and he would do what he had to do.

Gabe waited, crouched in the cover of the ferns, watching Elaine, taking in everything that happened in the clearing. Finally, one of the swampers stood and walked into the woods to Gabe's left. Gave moved silently through the brush. The man climbed up the hill a few feet and started tugging at his pants. Gabe stood up behind him, crooked one arm about the man's neck, and jerked his head three inches to the right. The swamper collapsed with a grunt, and Gabe lowered him to the ground. He pulled the man's pistol from his belt and checked the loads. Then he drew the tattered leather jacket on over his own and jammed the broad straw hat down low about his eyes. He dragged the dead man to better cover then walked down the hill to the clearing toward Elaine.

Everyone in camp was up and moving about. Some men squatted down before their fires to drink a cup of the tarry brew that passed for coffee in the Thicket. Others folded their

Snaketown

blankets into their packs and wiped the night's moisture from their weapons.

Gabe saw Caddo Jack was still busy with the horses. He couldn't find Lil but knew she was somewhere by the creek. As he reached Elaine, he kept his head down low, paused, and pretended to study the ground.

"Elaine, don't look up," he said softly. "Just keep your eyes somewhere else."

"Gabe? Oh my God, it's you!"

"Take it easy," Gabe said firmly. "Just sit there, all right? Don't pay any attention to me."

"I'll—I'll try, Gabe."

"You want to get us out of here in one piece, you better do more than try, Elaine. Now, I'm going to walk away some and look around. When you see me stop and scratch my face, you move. Get up slow, then take off running. Head for the trees right behind you. Don't look back at me, I'll be coming."

"Gabe—"

"Listen, Elaine. You'll hear some gunfire, but don't stop. The shots'll be coming from Jake Harper. He's up on that hill. Whatever you do, don't stop. You got all that?"

"Yes. I'm awful scared, Gabe."

"Good. Maybe that'll help your runnin' some."

Gabe walked off slowly, as if he were heading across the camp. Two men squatted by a cooking fire to his right.

"Bobby, we got some corn mush and some coffee if you want it," one of the men called out.

Gabe muttered something under his breath and kept going. The man clearly thought he was someone else, most likely the swamper he'd left back in the brush.

"Bobby, what the hell's wrong with you?" the other man yelled, "You deaf or something?"

"Hell with him," the first man grumbled. "He don't want breakfast, he can flat do without."

Gabe strolled around for another half a minute, then circled back toward Elaine, walking like a man still full of sleep. Everyone in camp seemed busy. No one seemed to notice he was there. Now, he thought, it's as good as it's going to get. Right now.

Someone let out a bloody yell by the creek. Gabe, along with everyone else in camp, stopped what they were doing and turned to stare.

Gabe figured the man was having a fit. He stood in the middle of the creek, churning up water, and jabbing his arm downstream. Half a dozen men from the clearing broke into a run and started for him. The man in the water shouted again, stopped, then jerked a big pistol from his belt and emptied it downstream.

"Now what?" Gabe muttered between his teeth. He turned quickly and looked at Elaine. She was on her feet now, staring fearfully at the creek.

"Go!" Gabe called to her. "Get out of here now!"

Elaine wouldn't move. A heavy volley of gunfire echoed from the creek. Gabe glanced at the stream then back to Elaine. "Do it!" he shouted. "What the hell are you waitin' for?"

"Mother," Elaine cried out, "oh Lord, she's down there by herself!"

Elaine darted past Gabe. He reached out to stop her as a swamper pushed him roughly aside and sent him sprawling.

Gabe came to his feet, cursing under his breath. Men were yelling at each other across the hollow, grabbing up their weapons, and rushing in confusion toward the creek.

Gabe tried to spot Elaine, but she was lost in the crowd. Riders suddenly exploded from the creek, their mounts kicking bright sprays of water in the air. They poured into the clearing, loosing a deadly hail of gunfire at the startled swampers.

Lead clipped Gabe's straw hat. A geyser of dirt erupted at his feet. He suddenly realized he looked like a man from the Thicket, that no one was likely to stop and ask his name. He threw the straw hat aside and ripped off the tattered jacket.

One of Lil's raiders turned and stared at Gabe, then reached for the pistol in his belt. A shot rang from the hill. The swamper looked surprised, then fell like a sack. Gabe waved a silent thanks to Harper and ran for the creek to find Elaine.

The clearing was full of riders. They cut through the ranks of the swampers like butter, killing them where they stood or riding them down. Gabe spotted John Marshall, then lost him again. A spotted gray broke through the riders, and Gabe saw

Robert Porter. He kicked his mount into the center of the fray. His eyes blazed, and his face was contorted in a terrible mask of rage. A bearded man cut at Porter's leg and tried to pull him from his mount. Porter swung his shotgun at the man and blew his face away.

A big man with a gator knife loomed in Gabe's path. Gabe shot him in the belly, raised his boot, and kicked the man aside. A horse knocked Gabe to the ground. Gabe rolled aside, stretched up, and grabbed the reins. The mount's rider was gone. Gabe threw himself into the saddle and kicked the frightened animal toward the creek.

The men from the Thicket were falling back. They had formed a ragged line, edging toward the safety of the woods. A few riders fell, but the men on the ground had little chance. Horses from the corral broke free and thundered wildly through the clearing, adding to the confusion of the fight.

Gabe saw John Marshall firing from the saddle to his left. A swamper went sprawling. Another went quickly to his knees and aimed his rifle at Marshall's head. Gabe jerked his horse to a halt and fired twice. The man cried out and went down. John raised his eyebrows in recognition and grinned at Gabe, then levered another shell into the chamber of his weapon.

Gabe bulled his mount through the crowd, searching for Elaine. His borrowed gun was empty. He bent low in the saddle and slashed out with his knife.

A shrill, unearthly cry cut through the early morning air. Gabe turned and saw Caddo Jack riding across the clearing, his legs pressed tightly against a wild-eyed horse. His face was stretched in a terrible grin, and he rode like a demon, swinging a long-handled axe with both hands. He burst through the riders, spilling men and mounts on either side. Men shouted and emptied their weapons at the phantom in their midst. Caddo Jack didn't stop. He rode straight for Robert Porter, without looking back.

Porter heard the awful cry and turned. Gabe saw his face go slack. Porter kicked his mount to one side, while he frantically tried to slip new shells into his gun. Caddo Jack was on him in an instant. He swung the long axe in a blur and struck Porter just above the eyes. The top of Porter's head disappeared,

severed as neatly as a melon. Caddo Jack rode on without stopping, crashing through the brush and into the trees beyond.

For a horrifying moment, Robert Porter sat straight in the saddle, a ghastly apparition spilling blood and gray matter from his skull, the beginning of a scream frozen forever on his lips. Then, he toppled over, the useless shotgun still gripped tightly in his hand.

A dozen riders emptied their weapons at the spot where Caddo Jack had vanished into the trees. Four of the men found the courage to follow him into the woods.

Gabe swung out of the saddle, splashing up to his knees in the creek. He searched about for Elaine, shouting out her name. Dead men floated in the water. He angrily shoved them aside. Dragging his feet through the current, he walked upstream, then cut back and started the other way.

John Marshall reined up on the bank, leaped down, and came in after Gabe.

"Damn it, she's got to be here," Gabe raged. "She has to be here, John!"

"We'll find her," Marshall said. "She's here, we're goin' to find her."

Gabe surged through the water until his feet wouldn't move. Finally, he staggered to the bank, sank down, and gasped for air. Marshall was beside him, but Gabe didn't see him at all. The world about him was tainted red with the anger that surged through his head.

When he stood and walked back to the clearing, men saw him and quickly moved aside. He looked at every dead man, thrusting his way through the horses and men. He found Holzer dead at the bottom of the hill. Jake Harper had shot him cleanly through the eye. Harper was pale and shaken. A man from the posse was trying to stop the flow of blood from his shoulder.

The fight had lasted less then four minutes. Eighteen men from Porter's bunch were dead, and twice as many hurt. Half of Lil's army was sprawled in the clearing, close to seventy-five men. The other half were gone. The search for the women went on until noon, but both Elaine and her mother had disappeared. It was almost as if the earth had opened up and swallowed them.

CHAPTER TWENTY-FIVE

Gabe let the boat drift across the dark water, past the grim columns of cypress bearded gray with moss. There was an unnatural stillness in the air, as if all the swarming life of the swamp had somehow suddenly disappeared. It was a moment when the Thicket went silent and held its breath between the daylight and the dark.

When the boat reached the shore, Gabe stepped out without a sound. He stood a long moment and listened. All he could hear was his own shallow breathing and the beat of his heart. Sitting in the shadow of a tree, he stripped off his shirt, then took off his boots. He laid these items in the bottom of the boat, then walked into the shallows. Scooping up mud from the bottom, he smeared the dark ooze over his body and his face. He picked up a clean bandanna from the boat and wiped two clean circles about his eyes. Finally, he took two fingers and ran them across his cheek and over the bridge of his nose to the other side. He picked up his knife and walked off into the shadows. Gabe Conrad was gone. It was Long Rider who sang a death song to himself, the harsh Lakota words ringing silently in his head.

Long Rider smelled the dry-sweet odor of the snakes before he saw them. He smelled the dead ashes of the fire, and

he smelled his enemy's sweat. Caddo Jack squatted on his haunches, tearing at a stringy piece of meat with his teeth. Lil sat in shadow nearby. Elaine was a few feet away. She sagged limply against a tree. Her arms were stretched tightly overhead, bound to a low branch. Her blouse was torn away, and her head hung over her bare breasts. Long Rider couldn't see her face.

Grasping the blade loosely in his hand, Long Rider stepped into the open. Lil cried out in alarm. Caddo Jack jerked his head up and stared. The half-breed looked as if he'd seen some terrible apparition from his dark and tortured dreams, a tall black demon with owl-like eyes and ragged stripes across his face. For an instant, Long Rider saw confusion in his eyes. Then, Caddo Jack grinned and came slowly to his feet.

"Knew I'd find you here," Long Rider said. "A rattler always goes back to his den."

The half-breed scowled at Long Rider. "You come to get her?"

"I came to kill you," Long Rider said.

Caddo Jack took a step to his right and jerked Elaine's head up by the hair. Elaine's mouth dropped open. Her eyes stayed closed. Her flesh was pale as death.

Caddo Jack laughed, loosed his grip on the girl, and turned to Long Rider. "You want the girl? You come and take her from Jack."

"That's what I'm going to do," Long Rider said softly.

Caddo Jack leaped across the snake pit and came at his foe in a blur, a knife flashing in his hand. Long Rider sucked in his belly and threw himself aside. The half-breed's blade whispered against his chest, stitching a line of blood.

Long Rider moved quickly to his right and thrust his knife at Caddo Jack's flesh. The blade struck home, scraping Caddo Jack's shoulder and slicing through flesh to bone. The half-breed grunted, turned the blade aside, and lashed out with the heavy hilt of his weapon. Long Rider staggered back. A branch struck his wrist and tore the knife from his hand. He hit the ground hard, and the air rushed out of his lungs.

Caddo Jack was on him at once, his dark features twisted in rage. His blade whipped down in a killing arc, nicking flesh

along Long Rider's ribs. Long Rider thrust his knee toward the half-breed's crotch. Caddo Jack saw it coming, twisted his leg aside to catch the blow, and struck Long Rider hard across the jaw.

Long Rider wasn't worried about the big man's fists. He could handle the blows and survive. It was the knife that would kill him. He had to get it away or he was dead.

The half-breed was bigger and stronger. It took everything Long Rider had to hold him off. Caddo Jack pounded him hard with his fists, while Long Rider fought to keep the knife from his throat. He clenched his teeth, ignoring the fists that threatened to pound his flesh into mush. He cried out and let his grip on the man's arm grow weak for an instant. Triumph flashed in Caddo Jack's eyes. He shifted his legs atop Long Rider's chest and raised his knife for a killing blow.

Long Rider brought all the strength he could muster to his shoulders and his chest, thrust his body up, twisted hard, and sent the half-breed sprawling.

Caddo Jack looked surprised. He came to his feet in a crouch, weaved to the left and right, then came at Long Rider with a vengeance. Long Rider backed off, searching the ground for his own weapon. Caddo Jack roared like a bull, hit Long Rider with his head, and drove him to the ground. Long Rider saw the knife flash in his hand and felt hot breath on his cheek. He kicked out roughly, forcing the half-breed back. Caddo Jack's knife lashed out, missed Long Rider, and sparked against stone. Long Rider rolled away. He spotted his own knife inches away in a cluster of ferns. He reached out desperately for the weapon. Caddo Jack grabbed his leg and held on. The half-breed laughed, striking out viciously, cutting at Long Rider's legs.

Long Rider bit back the pain, forced it from his mind. Another moment and Caddo Jack would kill him. He twisted to get away, kicking with his feet, but the half-breed held on with an iron grip. Long Rider lashed out with the leg that was free, caught the man's shoulder, and knocked him on his back. Long Rider turned and tried to bring himself erect. Nothing seemed to work. For an instant, fear knotted up in his belly. Caddo Jack had cut him bad. One leg was useless, and the

other wouldn't do him much good.

Caddo Jack came to his feet, shook his head, and looked at Long Rider. A broad grin spread across his features. He lifted his head to the sky and howled, waved his knife in the air, and came at Long Rider in a run.

Long Rider's hand touched the hilt of his own knife. He grasped the sharp edge with his fingers, whipped his arm straight out with all his strength, and let the blade fly.

Caddo Jack looked stunned. He stopped in his tracks, stared wide-eyed at Long Rider, then clawed at the knife buried deep in his belly. He staggered back, trying to pull the blade free. Lil screamed. The half-breed took another step and tumbled backwards into the pit.

Lil buried her face in her hands. Long Rider leaned back against a sapling and peered at his leg. He wiped away the mud and saw blood flowing freely from a wicked slash on his calf. Whipping off his belt, he wrapped the leather tightly about the wound, then pulled himself up. The bad leg worked, but he knew it wouldn't take him very far.

Gabe Conrad limped to Elaine and gently raised her head. Elaine moaned, opened her eyes for an instant, then passed out again.

Gabe turned on Lil. "What did that bastard do to her, Lil? What's wrong with her?"

"He hit her some," Lil said dully. "Elaine—got me away from the creek and all the shootin'. Jack found us—in the woods." She showed Gabe a weak smile. "He's good at gettin' what he wants. Elaine fought him some. Didn't want to go with him. Jack was plain crazy after . . ." Lil's voice trailed off.

"You saw it? What he did to Porter?"

Lil shook her head. "Me or Elaine, neither one did. He told us 'bout it, though. He had to do that." She looked up at Gabe. "He didn't do nothin' to her. I mean—what you was thinking. He was going to; I couldn't stop that."

"He's your creature," Gabe said harshly. "You made him what he was."

Lil didn't answer. For a long moment, she stared into the gathering dark. When she looked at Gabe again, he saw a sad, curious smile on her face.

"I'm part to blame, I know that. But it sure ain't all on my head. Robert's got to take some of that."

Gabe frowned. "What the hell does that mean?"

"Mean's what I said, that's what." Lil let out a breath. "I started hearin' the story when I first come back to the Thicket. Indian folks don't forget. Every Caddo around these parts knows what happened back then. A white man raped one of their girls and left her to die. Only she didn't die, mister. Not for a while. Not till she swole up and had a child."

Gabe stared. Something cold twisted up in his stomach. He didn't want to believe what he was thinking, but the truth was right there in the woman's eyes.

Lil grinned, and Gabe saw the flash of madness in her eyes. "Robert didn't know he had a son. I was savin' that for last. After I ruined him good, and Jack burned that damn town of his to the ground. I was goin' to let him know then."

"Did Jack know who he was? That he was Robert Porter's son?"

"Well 'course he did." Lil gave him a scornful look. "That's how I put the hate in him, taught him what it was he had to do." Lil laughed. "Lord, wouldn't ol' Robert have been surprised? Sure wish I could've seen that."

Gabe closed his eyes for a moment. "Lil. You didn't tell Elaine this, did you?"

"Why would I go and do that? Elaine's my own flesh and blood. I wouldn't do nothin' to hurt her for the world."

"Jack knew though," Gabe said grimly. "He knew that was his half sister there, and he was going to take her anyway. Lady, you've got a lot to answer for!"

"I never meant none of this to touch her. Most of the time the boy would listen to me, do what I told him to do. He kinda got worse, more'n I could handle. I didn't figure on that."

Lil paused and looked up at Gabe. "What you thinkin' on doin' with me? I reckon you'll give me to the law."

Gabe shook his head. "I don't give a damn about you," he said shortly. "I care what happens to her. She doesn't need any more hurt from you. If you're around, that's what she'll get."

Lil looked sadly at the rim of the darkened pit. "You shouldn't ought to just leave him like that. He wasn't much good to no one,

but he ought to get buried proper. He ought to have that."

Gabe looked narrowly at Lil. She had been a real pretty woman once, but she sure didn't look good anymore. She looked like a woman who'd eaten herself up with meanness inside.

"You want to bury him, get a shovel and start digging," Gabe said. "He looks just fine to me where he is."

EPILOGUE

Gabe found her in back of the white-columned house. She was wearing a blue calico gown and had her hair swept up atop her head. The garden was bright with roses, and she was down on her knees, snipping off the long-stemmed blossoms and setting them in a basket by her side.

She glanced up and smiled when Gabe appeared, stood, and ran into his arms. Gabe held her a moment and kissed her lightly on the cheek.

"You're looking right spry," Elaine said. "I'm real glad to see you walking well, Gabe."

"The leg's healed up fine," Gabe told her. "Can't keep a good man down."

Elaine smiled again. She nodded to the flowers on the ground. "I was cutting some roses. I—thought I might take some over to Jake."

"I just left him. He's getting meaner every day, so I guess that's a pretty good sign. His shoulder's going to heal up in time, if he doesn't haul off and hit someone first."

"Someone like you?"

"Yeah, someone like me."

Gabe studied the girl's face. "He's all right, Elaine. It pains

me to say it, but I can't help liking the man."

Elaine looked down at her hands. Gabe caught the look in her eyes, the faint rush of color at the mention of Jake Harper's name. He'd seen the look before several times and understood.

"Elaine." Gabe turned her chin up to face him. "Elaine, you don't have to play games with me, you ought to know that. You and me got real close. We care for each other, but there's got to be a lot more to it than that. You know it, and I know it, too."

Elaine looked away again. "I—guess I do." She laid her hands on Gabe's chest. "I don't know what I'll do, Gabe. Maybe there's something there between Jake and me. I guess I hope there is. I can't think real straight these days."

"You don't need to be thinking about anything now," Gabe told her. "You've been through a whole lot. Time's the only thing that's going to help that, Elaine. I know it for a fact."

"I think about mother a lot," Elaine said. "And father, too. Only sometimes I can't see their faces real clear. Why do you think that is? Why can't I see them anymore?"

" 'Cause your mind's trying to heal things up," Gabe said. "Things don't seem the same to you now as they will later on. You're going to have to give it time."

Elaine turned to him then, searching his eyes. She seemed to see something she hadn't seen before.

"You're telling me good-bye, aren't you? That's why you came."

"There's a boat going downriver this afternoon," Gabe said. "With any luck at all, it won't be the *Cypress Moon*."

"I know you have to go. I knew that all along. I'm not going to forget you, Gabe."

Gabe read the sadness, the touch of regret in her eyes. "I won't forget you either, Elaine."

She came into his arms and buried her head against his shoulder. He held her a long moment, neither of them speaking.

"Where will you go now?" she asked.

"Downriver. New Orleans, maybe. Somewhere else."

"Take care of yourself, Gabe Conrad."

"I'll try and do that," he said.

Gabe turned away then and walked up past the front of the big house, under the shaded streets toward town. A red-tailed hawk circled high up in the sky. He stopped a moment to watch and wondered if it might be the same one he'd seen in the Thicket. He thought about where it had been and what it might have seen from up there and where it might be going next.

Clay Dawson's
LONG RIDER

Born to settler parents, raised an Indian, he was caught between the blood and hate of his two peoples—living by his own code in a land where death came quick and vengeance could last a lifetime...

___	#4 APACHE DAWN	1-55773-195-0/$2.95
___	#5 KILL CRAZY HORSE!	1-55773-221-3/$2.95
___	#6 SHADOW WAR	1-55773-252-3/$2.95
___	#7 THE GHOST DANCERS	1-55773-279-5/$2.95
___	#9 THE LAND BANDITS	1-55773-316-3/$2.95
___	#10 THE BUFFALO HUNTERS	1-55773-335-X/$2.95
___	#11 THE SANTA FE RING	1-55773-354-6/$2.95
___	#12 KILLER MUSTANG	1-55773-389-9/$2.95
___	#13 VENGEANCE TOWN	1-55773-428-3/$2.95
___	#14 THE COMMANCHEROS	1-55773-480-1/$2.95
___	#15 BLOOD HUNT	1-55773-528-8/$2.95

For Visa, MasterCard and American Express orders ($10 minimum) call: 1-800-631-8571

Check book(s). Fill out coupon. Send to:
BERKLEY PUBLISHING GROUP
390 Murray Hill Pkwy., Dept. B
East Rutherford, NJ 07073

NAME_____

ADDRESS_____

CITY_____

STATE _____ ZIP_____

PLEASE ALLOW 6 WEEKS FOR DELIVERY.
PRICES ARE SUBJECT TO CHANGE
WITHOUT NOTICE.

POSTAGE AND HANDLING:
$1.50 for one book, 50¢ for each additional. Do not exceed $4.50.

BOOK TOTAL $_____

POSTAGE & HANDLING $_____

APPLICABLE SALES TAX $_____
(CA, NJ, NY, PA)

TOTAL AMOUNT DUE $_____

PAYABLE IN US FUNDS.
(No cash orders accepted.)

205c

Also in the LONG RIDER Series from Diamond

LONG RIDER
FAST DEATH
GOLD TOWN
APACHE DAWN
KILL CRAZY HORSE!
SHADOW WAR
THE GHOST DANCERS
HELLHOLE
THE LAND BANDITS
THE BUFFALO HUNTERS
KILLER MUSTANG
THE SANTA FE RING
VENGEANCE TOWN
THE COMANCHEROS
BLOOD HUNT

AN UNANNOUNCED VISITOR

Gabe sat up straight as someone began to hammer violently on the cabin door. The thin panel shook as if a mule were kicking it with his foot.

"Whatever you want," Gabe called out, "that's not the way to get it. Knock decent, friend, and you might get a decent answer."

At the sound of Gabe's words, the kicking ceased at once. A man began to curse at the top of his lungs. Half a second later, lead ripped through the door, splintering wood and letting daylight into the room.